# THE LADY AND THE SPY

## The Ladies of Sommer-by-the-Sea
### Book 2

## Ruth A. Casie

## ARE YOU SIGNED UP FOR DRAGONBLADE'S BLOG?

You'll get the latest news and information on exclusive giveaways, exclusive excerpts, coming releases, sales, free books, cover reveals and more.

Check out our complete list of authors, too!

No spam, no junk. That's a promise!

### Sign Up Here

www.dragonbladepublishing.com

*Dearest Reader;*

*Thank you for your support of a small press. At Dragonblade Publishing, we strive to bring you the highest quality Historical Romance from some of the best authors in the business. Without your support, there is no 'us', so we sincerely hope you adore these stories and find some new favorite authors along the way.*

*Happy Reading!*

*CEO, Dragonblade Publishing*

# Additional Dragonblade books by Author Ruth A. Casie

**The Ladies of Sommer-by-the-Sea Series**
The Lady and Her Quill (Book 1)
The Lady and the Spy (Book 2)

**Pirates of Britannia Series**
Donald
Hugh
Graham
The Pirate's Jewel
The Pirate's Redemption

# CHAPTER ONE

*February 14, 1815*
*Sommer-by-the-Sea*

L ADY PATRICE MONTGOMERY Edgemont, young widow of the late Lord Benedict Edgemont, 3rd Earl of Gosforth entered The Rostov Tearoom. She was home in Sommer-by-the-Sea, permanently. Her extended stay in London was a distant memory and she had every intention to keep it that way.

She stomped her feet to remove the slush from her boots and brushed the snow from her primrose yellow pelisse. After wearing black for ten months, she swore she'd never wear the color again.

This snowstorm was as unexpected as her early return. She shouldn't have left, but in a moment of uncharacteristic weakness her mother won the day.

"You'll stay in London with your father and me. You shouldn't be alone mourning your loving husband."

Loving husband. That sounded well and good, but she felt no need to mourn over something that didn't exist.

A year and a day. Really? Two weeks' mourning was more than enough. But after several arguments, Patrice relented. She closed her country home, The Mooring, in Sommer-by-the-Sea with plans to reopen it in April when her year and one day was over. But that didn't suit her mother either.

"One doesn't rusticate in the country until the end of the Season, in June." As if she didn't know. Like a relentless woodpecker, Lady Montgomery nagged, jabbed, and stabbed away until Patrice threw her hands in the air and gave in. She'd return north the first of July.

But after last week's final indignity she refused to stay in London a moment longer. Without a word to anyone, she packed herself up and with her lady's maid, Jean, returned to Sommerby-the-Sea. A year and a day. The end of the Season be damned.

She arrived two days ago with her bags in hand at Marianna Ravencroft's doorstep to a surprised but warm welcome.

The coach ride had been brutal, but the shock on Anna's face when she entered the parlor was priceless. Anna quickly rallied. It didn't take long before they were once again sharing a room as they had at Mrs. Bainbridge's Sommer-by-the-Sea Female Seminary.

Removing the last of the snow from her boots, Patrice soaked up the familiar tearoom that bustled with activity. After staring at the drab furnishings at Montgomery Hall, she thrilled at seeing the painted blue walls with blue damask wallpaper insets in white wainscot panels. She looked across the neat rows of tables, each dressed in a crisp white linen cloth with a lace overlay. Small vases filled with a bouquet of red quince, winter heather, and white snowdrops added a soft and bright finishing touch to the room.

Patrice took a deep breath and enjoyed the grassy aroma of green tea and the astringent scent of the black variety along with the mouth-watering fragrance of warm bread, and sweet scones. The turmoil of the last year slid away. She felt lighter, her spirits brighter. Restored.

The server passed with a tureen of soup. The savory fragrance of the tearoom's signature mushroom barley soup stirred memories best left buried deep in the St. Petersburg snow. She blinked and quickly squashed the budding images before they could develop.

As bundled as she was, a chill crossed her shoulders and up her neck. It was an uneasy, unnerving, under-scrutiny feeling. A warning voice went off in her head, someone was watching. She glanced to her right. Tatiana Chernokov, proprietress of the tearoom, was actively engaged in a discussion with a gentleman.

*Gentleman* may have been an overstatement. A further glance had Patrice appalled that Tanya allowed the man into the tearoom and had not directed him to the kitchen door. She was a kind soul, and well thought of by the *ton*. This man could be her downfall.

Tanya's back was to her. The man faced Patrice and stared at her intently.

She took a better look. While his appearance was more "vagabond" than "gentleman," it was his clothes that appeared out of place, not the man. From his loose black trousers, snug white shirt, fitted brown waistcoat, to his broad-brimmed gray hat, it was clear to her he wore the wrong costume.

He had a rugged look with a full beard, and long, curly hair pulled back in a romantic, wild way. But his fixed gaze held her captive. His compelling eyes were summer-sky blue and oddly familiar. Could she have met him before?

He smiled and tilted his head in an arrogant yet elegant nod. Her heart jumped in her chest. The excitement had her heart racing.

Tanya turned, a surprised expression on her face, and gave Patrice a wave. She nodded, leaving Tanya and the man to figure out which of them she acknowledged. Even she wasn't certain.

She did have to admit the man was appealing.

Her mother would have a convulsion if she had a hint of her daughter's thoughts. She bit her cheek to stifle her smile. Poor Mother would never understand attraction. Position, title, assets, and gossip were the things that drove her.

Patrice glanced around the room and found her friends seated at a back table. They were a close group of graduates from Mrs.

Bainbridge's who met weekly, either at the tearoom or the seminary's salon.

As she made her way to her friends, she tried to figure out where she had encountered the man. Nothing came to mind. It was useless at the moment. She would remember sooner or later.

Patrice didn't know if she was annoyed or pleased that the only empty chair faced Tanya and the man. She avoided looking at him and chatted with her friends. When she did look up, she was once again caught in his snare. The audacity. God's toes, was she destined to be attracted to a rake in any clothing? It had certainly proved to be her pattern of late.

She dragged her glance away and immediately felt a void, an emptiness. Ridiculous. What was she, some naïve schoolgirl whose head could be easily turned? And by whom? She placed her reticule on her lap all the while schooling herself not to look at the doorway.

"Welcome home." Hattie grabbed her hand and gave it a squeeze. "I was taken aback when Anna told us you had returned. We didn't expect you until July."

Effie placed a scone on Patrice's plate and took one for herself. "Is it true you're home to stay?"

"I enjoyed being here for the Harvest Festival in November. I missed you all terribly and I am past the stage of residing in my parents' home."

"I was surprised you went to stay with your parents." Effie poured Patrice a cup of hot tea. "Your London address is a perfectly grand home."

Anna nudged Patrice. "Who are you staring at?"

Patrice gave Anna a shocked glare while Hattie and Effie glanced toward the doorway.

"Who is he?" Effie's voice was soft, almost playful, her tone conspiratorial.

*God's big toe.* She was staring at him, again. Something in the back of her mind kept poking her. She couldn't fit the man with a place. She casually turned toward her friends.

"You'll have to ask Tanya. He does appear familiar, but I can't place him. He must remind me of someone. But I have no idea who." Had she seen him in passing somewhere along her journey? The road, the inn, someplace? Patrice placed the linen serviette on her lap, her mind not letting go of the puzzle.

"What were they saying? You were standing next to them." Effie picked up a scone and slathered it with raspberry jam.

"Effie." Patrice sounded indignant, but her mood quickly cooled. "My Russian is rusty. I didn't get much past 'What are you doing here?' They spoke too quickly for me."

"You can ask Tanya, if you dare." Something flicked across Hattie's face. "I love Tanya, but she's like my mother. She and my grandmother speak German when they don't want any of us to understand what they're saying. Including my father."

"You know your father speaks fluent German." Patrice glanced at the ceiling with a someone-give-me-strength look. "So does everyone else in your family."

"You know that, and I know that, but Mother? No." Hattie could hardly keep the laughter out of her voice. "I asked her once and she proudly told me that father has many talents, but speaking a foreign language was not one of them. Which made me laugh. And yes, Father taught my sister and me German, with instructions never to tell Mother."

"So much for your mother's private talks." Patrice lifted her teacup in a salute.

"That's all very enlightening. But that's not what I want to talk about." Hattie's expression went serious. "We said little when you were home in November, but we've all been concerned about you since…"

Patrice leaned toward Hattie and covered her friend's hand with her own. "Edgemont's passing was difficult to bear. Thank you, and I say that with all my heart. Your letters kept me sane at a time when madness surrounded me. The *ton* can be so cruel." Even she heard the sneer in her voice.

"I never thought the gossip or scandal sheets were harmful,

simply entertaining." Hattie's declaration didn't surprise Patrice. She would have agreed if she wasn't their target.

"Of course you wouldn't. Their so-called polite conversations are verbal duels, fencing matches. I refuse to thrust and parry for groups of spectators. I prefer an intimate dagger attack. Swift, clean, and done."

Patrice's thoughts randomly jumped to last year's trip to St. Petersburg. She'd been pleasantly surprised when she and her husband traveled with Ambassador Cathcart to St. Petersburg. Had it been only ten months since that voyage? It seemed like a lifetime ago.

Edgemont's intentions for an evening with her alone may have been well-intentioned, but as pleasant, witty, and likeable as her husband was, he couldn't keep a promise, at least not to her.

Her husband's pained expression when he was called to a meeting was little consolation. Intellectually, she understood business came first. Emotionally, it was disappointing. Graciously, Prince Baranov came to the rescue and played her escort to the ballet and dinner.

How odd. She hadn't thought of that evening with the prince in some time.

Effie's chatter brought her back to the present.

"I'm sorry, Effie, what were you saying?" Patrice poured a cup of tea, passed up the sugar Anna offered, and took a splash of milk.

"I was shocked when I read your letter. How dare someone ask for the name of your husband's mistress." Effie's choice of topic would have left a deep wound had she not been one of Patrice's good friends. With these women, nothing was censored.

"Perhaps the gossip columnist is afraid her husband is on the market for a mistress." Anna folded and unfolded her linen serviette, her expression worried and wary.

Effie stabbed her fork into a tart. "I still can't believe the mistress's husband killed—"

"Effie." Hattie poked her elbow into Effie's side. "Patrice is sitting right here."

"Oh, Patrice." Effie dropped her fork. "I didn't mean to hurt you."

"Please, you know my marriage was not a love match. We knew each other since we were children. It seemed the natural course of events, but it was an arrangement. A mistress? None of his friends were aware of any liaisons. At least that is what they felt compelled to tell me." The words stuck in her throat like a dry piece of bread she couldn't get down. "It's strange. I didn't think he would ever… it doesn't matter now." She threw her shoulders back and held her head high. "I shouldn't have been surprised."

That wasn't the truth. She was incredibly surprised. There had been affection between them, but love? Not the type that takes your breath away when you heard his voice. Not the type that made your heart jump out of your chest when you saw him. Not that type at all. And if there was no emotional bond between them, why did his betrayal hurt her so?

Once again she felt the uncertainty and instability of his passing. The pain of his infidelity. The endless days of numbness that turned into anger.

Anna poured the last drops of tea into her cup. She opened the teapot and glanced inside. "Oh dear, the pot is empty."

"The tarts are gone as well." Effie held up the empty plate. "You can refresh the tea while I get more tarts." Effie turned to Hattie and Patrice. "We'll be back."

Hattie slid her chair a bit closer to Patrice. "You know you can tell us everything. There have never been any secrets between any of us. You know we are not those London women telling secrets to whomever is willing to listen."

Patrice didn't doubt Hattie's sincerity, nor that of the others. Slowly, the guard she had cemented in place gave way.

"Your letters and Mrs. Bainbridge's books and articles, even the ones about Napoleon, were a distraction from those difficult times. For weeks Edgemont's murder and his widow were fodder for the *ton*. It was the one time I was grateful for mother's insistence that I do not accept callers."

"Except George Armstrong?"

"Mother treated him as staff, and to her, staff aren't people of concern." Patrice let out a strangled laugh that sounded more strained than pleasant. "Mr. Armstrong was a businessman who worked with my father. We were each relegated to specific rooms at specific times, so we didn't disturb the running of the house or Mother's afternoon court. I only saw him in passing and when I did, we never spoke.

"It was Mother who led to us becoming acquainted. She had an early caller and pushed me into the library. Imagine my surprise when I found it occupied by Mr. Armstrong. I stood there like a timid mouse, not able to go back the way I came, my only escape through the garden door.

"He was quick to point out the library was big enough for a grand ball, let alone two people reading. I remember how his gentle voice dipped low, his apologetic tone filled with caring, closeness, concern. It was as if he interrupted me.

"Up until then, I hadn't gotten more than a passing glance of his straight blonde hair. I couldn't have told you the color of his eyes. Now I took a good look. He was pleasant to look at, dressed as he was in the latest fashion with a polished look of an accomplished gentleman. He wore a hunter green morning coat over a white linen shirt with a patterned cravat, and soft white leather breeches."

"And his eyes? What color were they?"

Patrice glanced at Anna. "Dark brown, so dark they could be mistaken for black." A bubble of a laugh burst out of her mouth.

"Patrice, that's not fair. You're in your head. Let me in. What has you wondering off?"

"It's nothing, Hattie. Something Mr. Armstrong said."

"Oh, no. You will not keep that to yourself."

"If you must know, when we discussed sharing the room, he likened himself to a goldfish."

Hattie pulled back a bit, her mouth gaping open.

"Much like you look at the moment." Patrice finished the last of her tea and tried to hide her smile. "Armstrong mentioned that his lips moved when he read, like a goldfish. I was stunned by his absurd statement, the image of his cheeks pressed together and lips moving like a fish had me laughing so hard I wasn't able to stop." Patrice took on a more serious attitude.

"The more I laughed, the more something deep inside me fought to be free. Free to feel, free to smile, free to live. I couldn't keep it locked away any longer. I let it loose, and I felt…" Patrice searched for the word.

"Alive?"

Patrice was too startled by Hattie's suggestions to say anything.

"All from imagining Mr. Armstrong's goldfish lips."

"If he helped you through your grief, and have no illusions, you *were* grieving, I would think he was a wonderful man."

"He was at first. He was attentive and thoughtful. For weeks I was a ghost in my parents' house – dejected, neglected, overprotected. His words had my heart racing like a thoroughbred, yet all I wanted was to sprint from the room."

"Why? He sounds like a good man."

"His smile was warm, yet made me feel exposed, a touch uncomfortable."

"You know what you want. Don't be afraid of it when it's within your grasp." Hattie always did have a positive outlook. But if only she knew. There were times when you reached for something, and you were burned.

"How can I be sure? I thought I knew Edgemont."

"You're an intelligent woman. Don't let anyone tell you otherwise. You were giddy about Mr. Armstrong when you were here for the festival."

"My parents encouraged the relationship. We spent many afternoons together. He gave me a gift." Patrice settled her breath while Hattie was so excited, she nearly jumped out of her chair.

"A deck of playing cards. He said he saw them and thought of me."

Hattie gasped and reached a comforting hand toward Patrice.

"Exactly. I thought it was some cruel joke. Surely he knew my brother had been shot dead over a card game at a gambling den. The *ton* enjoyed that bit of gossip on the heels of Edgemont's murder. What other reason would *cards* bring me to mind." Patrice covered the comforting hand with her own. "I didn't mean to upset you. It wasn't that at all. It was the picture of a bouquet of flowers on the back that had attracted him."

"That's a relief. He had a simple explanation. You are still too sensitive to Brian's passing. I don't see why you were so off put by Mr. Armstrong."

"Sorry we took so long." Effie took her seat. "Tanya will bring the tarts when they are ready."

Anna freshened everyone's tea. "Careful, it's hot."

"Pass me the milk, please." Effie held her hand out. "Did you have a difficult time reaching Sommer-by-the-Sea? It seems this snow has been falling for days."

Patrice was thankful she changed the subject.

"It wasn't snowing in London when I left. The coach was rather comfortable until we reached Harrogate. I woke on the last day of our journey to a blizzard. A day's ride turned into two days. It made me think of how we turned Mrs. Bainbridge's garden into a battlefield, each of us wearing a red wool cap, and tossing snow at each other."

"Those were good times." Anna laughed. "I hadn't thought of those days in a long time."

"What hadn't you thought about?" Tanya approached carrying a bundle that she put on the empty table behind her and a dish of tarts she put in front of Effie.

"Winter days in the seminary garden when we used the snow as a good excuse to attack each other, then take turns sliding down the steep slope on a carpet. Patrice was the best at sliding. She took us into her icehouse. We had turns going down the ramp." Effie helped herself to a chocolate tart.

"Until Brian told my father, who was very upset with us. I hadn't thought of that adventure in a long time." Patrice smiled softly and had another sip of tea.

"Somehow I cannot imagine you ladies sliding on the ice or tossing snow at each other." Tanya smiled. "Although, I did the same with my brother in St. Petersburg. He always let me win."

"Are you sure you're not giving him more credit than he deserves?" Patrice said.

"No, not at all. My aim was laughable. I tossed the snow, missed him, but he fell down no matter where the snowball landed."

"You must have a sweet brother. Mine put stones in his snowballs and threw them at everyone, especially me," Patrice said. "He was not sweet. To him, winning was everything. It eventually was his undoing."

"Alicia was the best at throwing snowballs." Patrice wondered if Anna purposefully moved the conversation along. "And Patrice was our commander. She would do anything to win and usually did. Everyone wanted to be on her team, but we complained. She had you digging holes in the deep snow to make traps, rigging branches to slap the enemy down, and covering patches of ice with snow so they'd slip."

"I remember coming inside after we were thoroughly exhausted and cold. Mrs. Bainbridge would have hot chocolate and biscuits ready for us, along with towels she kept warm by the hearth." Effie looked at the fresh tarts and debated. "These are heart shaped. How lovely. For Valentine's Day?"

"They're my Valentine to you." Tanya picked up the plate and passed it along.

"We have Valentines to share as well." Anna removed a neatly folded paper from her reticule. "Ladies, put them into the center of the table and we'll each take one. Patrice, you go first."

"Anna, aren't we going to wait for the others?" Patrice asked.

"Dorothea sent word she wouldn't be joining us. Her father

was called away and she is seeing to his office. Katherine is still in Bath. I'm afraid it is Hattie, Effie and me."

The ladies took out intricately folded pieces of paper, each with *Be My Valentine* carefully penned on the front.

Patrice took her Valentine out of her reticule. The ritual started out as a game she introduced to them. As children she, Brian, and Edgemont folded paper intricately to hide messages. They would exchange them and see who could figure out the proper way to get to the hidden message. There was only one way to begin. Find that key fold and the rest was easy.

The memory brought her up short. Those early days when she and Brian were close, when they cared about each other, what had become of them? By the time she understood what was happening to him it was too late to help him, protect him. He wasn't strong enough to protect himself against their mother.

Her early interference was the reason she was sent to the seminary. Out of the house. Out of Brian's life. Her visits home were painful. The Brian she adored was gone. The man he became was nothing like the sweet loving boy she knew.

What good was reliving the past? It couldn't be changed. She blinked away the memory and directed her thoughts to the present.

"While you make delicious treats," Patrice held up her Valentine, "we write special poems for each other to enjoy."

"But I don't have one to share with you." Tanya stared at the folded paper and chewed her lip.

"I brought two. You must sit down, in Dorothea's seat, or you will fall down swooning. We take our Valentines very seriously. We have a simple process. You choose a Valentine from the center of the table, read it out loud, then pick who reads next."

Tanya took the vacant seat, chose a Valentine, and worked carefully to open it. Patrice watched as she glanced at the message. Tanya raised her head, a smile across her face.

*"The rose is red, the violet's blue,*
*The honey's sweet, and so are you.*
*Thou are my love, and I am thine.*
*I drew thee to my Valentine:*
*The lot was cast and then I drew,*
*And Fortune said it should be you."*

"The drawing is wonderful." She turned it around to show the others a picture of a bouquet of roses. "The sentiment and the roses are both very lovely." Tanya looked around the table. "Anna, you're next."

Anna's hand hovered over the pile and finally settled on a paper. She unfolded it and read.

*"Beneath the rose there you will find*
*A pleasing subject to your mind*
*See virtuous courtship, calm repose.*
*It's innocent, yet, under the rose."*

"I so look forward to these verses," Anna said. "This is the only way I'm ever going to get a Valentine and I'm happy it's from you." She around the table. "Effie, you're next."

Effie chose one of the three remaining papers and unfolded it.

*"May we dear youth together prove.*
*The bliss and joy of faithful love.*
*And may true love our hearts entwine.*
*On this best day of Valentine."*

Patricia pasted a benign smile on her face. Virtuous courtship was one thing, but faithful love was a dream. It only existed in Valentine verses or in stories. She was glad her friends were enjoying themselves, but for her, the holiday was empty.

Hattie took the next to the last paper on the table.

> *"The rose is fairest when it's budding new*
> *The rose is sweetest washed with morning dew*
> *Hope is brightest when drawn from fears*
> *And love is loveliest when embalmed with tears."*

"This is a charming tradition, exchanging Valentines." Tanya examined the note.

"I agree. We don't need to wait for some gentleman to send them. We can exchange Valentines with each other," Effie said.

"I wrote this on my way from London, for Mr. Armstrong." Patrice opened the last paper.

> *"You stupid vain conceited fool,*
> *Why ogle and wantonly drool.*
> *I'm sure no damsel will incline,*
> *To choose you for her Valentine."*

"You didn't give that to him, did you?" Effie wasn't the only one shocked by her Valentine. "He would not find it funny."

"In November you said your parents were all for him. What changed their mind?" Anna folded her Valentine and put it in her reticule.

"What makes you think they are the ones with the changed mind? I imagine they are quite cross with me."

"What did you do? We've been very patient. We expected to read the engagement announcement when you returned to London in November. Instead, three months later you're at Anna's doorstep."

"It's not what I did, but what George Armstrong did, or more correctly what he didn't do. When I returned to London in November he was nowhere to be seen. Mr. Armstrong was gone."

"Oh dear, I thought…" Effie's shocked face melted into concern. "If he was gone, why did your father call you back to London?"

"There were rumors Edgemont's holdings were expected to collapse. The company's solicitor Joseph Peters refused to tell my father anything, so I went to see him.

"Mr. Peters sat behind Edgemont's desk and blamed the failing on my husband's poor management. He was surprised but cooperative when I asked to see the accounts. His broad grin that showed his very straight white teeth was gracious, but I didn't believe him for one minute. He didn't count on me understanding the documents. I have been managing my trust for some time and have done a good job of it. I assure you reviewing Edgemont's accounts was enlightening."

"Men can be so thickheaded," Hattie said.

"I left his office and hired a new solicitor at once, Hughes, Swift, and Lacey." She turned to Anna. "I have your father to thank. I remembered him speaking about the firm on more than one occasion. I took the liberty of mentioning your father's name. Mr. Lacey saw me at once. Three weeks later he reported that they found some unscrupulous activity in handling Edgemont's accounts after his passing. They were all executed by Peters. In other words, he stole from the business."

"Then Joseph Peters was the JP mentioned in the papers as having been ruined by the dead," Hattie said. "Father remarked at dinner just the other day that JP was begging for business. I never thought to ask him the identity of JP."

"I did not ruin Mr. Peters. He ruined himself. By removing him I was able to secure and stabilize the business. With Mr. Lacey's help, I took an active role in Edgemont's business and spent the last two months turning it to right. We were able to restore the stolen funds and property. Since then, I've overseen the business. My new solicitor was able to keep my involvement discreet."

Everyone was silent.

Patrice drank her tea, managing to maintain a façade of indifference.

"Mr. Armstrong returned to London last week." Patrice

tossed out the words and waited for her friends to react.

"Returned? Did he tell you where he had been?" Effie was always full of questions.

"Why he left without a word?" Anna asked.

"That's why you're here," Tanya added. "You didn't stay to see him."

"No." She put her teacup down. "I did not. I was told Mr. Armstrong and my father made inquiries into Edgemont's business. Thankfully, Mr. Lacey directed them both to me. I believe that is why Mr. Armstrong was at Montgomery Hall asking my father for my hand." Patrice dismissively waved her hand. She held her head high. "He's not interested in me. It's Edgemont's very successful business he wants."

She took a sip of the tepid tea as the sting of reality washed over her. "I saw no reason to stay in London." Her tone was as matter-of-fact as her words. But inside, she was anything but calm.

In November, she traveled to Sommer-by-the-Sea for the Harvest Festival and to support another of Mrs. Bainbridge graduate's, her friend Lady Alicia Hartley, who was reading her new book at Mrs. Miller's Circulating Library.

She planned to stay with her friends longer than a fortnight but returned to London after receiving a message from her father. In truth, she looked forward to telling Mr. Armstrong about her adventure.

The carriage had barely stopped when she got out and dashed into the house, expecting some sort of welcome. There was none. She pulled off her gloves and removed her hat as she hurried into the library. Empty. She went through the adjoining door to the drawing room.

There she found her father and Joseph Peters, the Edgemont solicitor. She glanced around the room, but no one else was there.

In her heart of hearts, she knew Mr. Armstrong was gone.

Her father sat her down and with Mr. Peters began to make

demands. Something about Edgemont's finances near collapse.

She barely heard what they said. She used all her energy to breathe. When she had enough, she got up and left the room leaving her father and Peters speechless.

Two weeks went by without any word from Mr. Armstrong.

His sudden absence in London led to more gossip. Some she simply couldn't ignore.

"I noticed Mr. Armstrong has been absent of late," she said to her father, while she had her soup at dinner.

"Bright young man. We finished our dealings. Yes, a bright young man."

Was that all her father had to say? She turned to her mother.

"He was a pleasant diversion, I'm sure. Not the sort of man a woman of your stature commands."

"Oh, that's surprising. According to today's gossip it was the other way around, I was found to be beneath him."

Her father nearly choked on his bisque. In a fit of rage, he threw down his serviette and bellowed.

She turned to him, an over exaggerated look of surprise on her face.

"I don't understand why you're upset. That's what was said. Lady Ashcroft sat in our drawing room this afternoon while Mother announced it loud enough when she played court with several others." She turned to her mother who looked horrified.

The coldness in Patrice's eyes made her mother flinch. "You and the other women… laughed."

Patrice put down her soup spoon and placed her serviette on the table. "I have a headache. If you'll excuse me, I'll take the remainder of my dinner in my room."

"Patrice, come back here," her mother demanded. "It was simply the play on words that was—"

"Indecent, insulting, inexcusable." Patrice glanced over her shoulder at her mother. "And hurtful."

There was no need to hear her mother's explanation. Nothing she said could make it better. It was her mother's voice she heard make the comment. It was her mother's distinctive laugh that carried out into the hall. It was her mother's friends who tried to quiet her in case someone else would hear. No, there was nothing her mother could say that would make it better.

"I'm sure the topic was the talk of your friend's tables this evening. I wonder how that sat with their husbands and the impact on Father's reputation, what little he has left after Brian."

"How dare you speak of your brother—"

"You mean the brother that nearly bankrupted Father and tore his reputation to shreds. Oh, yes, that brother." Patrice paused. "May he rest in peace. God knows, he's given us none."

As she made her way up the stairs the entire house listened to her father's tirade, her mother trying to explain.

Patrice almost prayed for someone else to befall some great disaster so the focus would move away from her. She went to her room and counted the days until her return to Sommer-by-the-Sea.

The following day her mother was too ill to come downstairs although she managed to visit Lady Ashcroft early, before the usual calling hour. Patrice, on the other hand, was once again a prisoner in her parents' home.

As weeks turned into months, she gave up any hope that Mr. Armstrong would return or send word. Perhaps she had misread his intentions. He hadn't taken any liberties. Not that he didn't try. There were plenty of playful insinuations.

Autumn slowly turned to winter. The trees in the garden were bare. The flowers were long gone. The days were gray and cold.

She stared out her bedroom window. Four more months and she'd return to Sommer-by-the-Sea. Tomorrow would have been her third wedding anniversary. It was difficult to think that only last year she and Edgemont had traveled to St. Petersburg. She had such hopes for the trip. It started with promise but ended in total disaster.

The clopping of horses' hooves stopping in front of their door drew her attention. It was too early for callers.

George Armstrong stepped down from the carriage and went to the door.

Her heart didn't skip a beat. Her head didn't swim with anticipation. She was past being angry and all the way to indifferent.

Without any need to see him, she returned to her chair by the hearth and picked up the essay Mrs. Bainbridge had sent to her about the attributes of Napoleon Bonaparte. She had been reading for a half hour when her mother burst into her room.

"How wonderful. Your father is speaking with Armstrong. I told you to be patient. He's come to offer for you. Come to the drawing room."

She stared at her mother as if she were daft.

"Mother, you were very clear that he was—" She chose her words carefully. "Not the man for me. Why is he speaking to Father? I'm a widow and responsible for myself. Shouldn't he be speaking with me? And marriage? I haven't seen or heard from him in months." She went back to her reading. "Marriage. He mentioned nothing before his absence. If he should ask, tell him I'm not taking callers today. The audacity of the man."

"That's not true. He spoke to your father in the summer and again in November." Her mother drew in a sharp breath. "Come to the drawing room."

Patrice said nothing. She didn't move, didn't flinch, didn't breathe.

Her mother, unable to look her in the eye, twisted her handkerchief into knots and gave her a smile that was more grimace and ready for an argument than a discussion.

Still Patrice said nothing. She learned a long time ago silence was her best weapon.

"While you were up north." Her mother stopped playing with the piece of linen and finally looked at her.

Patrice lowered the papers. Her mother was saying something but all she heard was the thunder of her own heartbeat.

"Father did what?" She glared at her mother. Slowly she got

to her feet. "What have you both been up to?"

"Don't give me that look. He came to your father in the spring about Edgemont's financial situation. As dismal as it was he still asked for your hand. I told them both, dear Edgemont wasn't cold in his grave. It was only months since he passed. You couldn't think of marrying at the time. No, not for a year and one day." Her mother wagged her finger. "It was out of the question."

"Why wasn't I told? And why was father talking about Edgemont's business? He has no control over it. I do. And what gave you or Father the right to interfere between Mr. Armstrong and me? I'm no longer—"

"You had been so distraught. Your father and Armstrong were doing what was best."

"For whom? Certainly not me."

"It's Mr. Armstrong that turned Edgemont's company around. I overheard him mention a new solicitor he engaged, a Mr. Lacey."

"He engaged?" Her voice was raised. "He did no such thing. Mr. Lacey works for me. I hired him. I pay him. I make all the decisions for the company."

"Mr. Armstrong did mention that he needed you to speak to Mr. Lacey. I don't see why. You know nothing about how to run a business. If your brother were alive—"

"I'd be bankrupt. All Brian knew how to do was wheedle money out of you and cheat others out of theirs and gamble it away. He was most proficient at that. He did it so well he got himself killed. Shot in the head."

Her mother gave her a horrified look. "This is why your father and Mr. Armstrong stepped in. You're too emotional. You're still upset about Edgemont's passing. It certainly wasn't time for you to remarry. You wait here," her mother said over her shoulder as she hurried toward the door. Patrice wasn't sure if it was to get away from her or to reach father and Mr. Armstrong.

"I'll tell your father you'll be down shortly." Her mother stopped her hand on the latch and turned. "No, not so quickly. I think thirty minutes possibly forty-five would be best. He made you wait what was it dear, three months." She smiled and was gone.

Married. To George Armstrong. And how dare he speak to Mr. Lacey.

The Napoleon essay abandoned, she placed a bookmark on the page, and noticed a sentence that the headmistress had marked.

*"Take time to deliberate, but when the time for action has arrived, stop thinking and go."*

Stop thinking and go. Indeed. Patrice stared at the door for several heartbeats deliberating, then tucked the papers back into the folio.

"Thank you, Mrs. Bainbridge. I've been doing what everyone else wants, listening to the innuendos, thoughtless comments, sitting by idly, removed instead of involved. I should have done this months ago."

Twenty minutes later, the staff was shocked into silence when she and Jean entered the servants' hall carrying their luggage.

"Lady Edgemont. I wasn't aware you were leaving today," Mr. Carter, the butler, looked at her portmanteau.

"It has been a long time coming. The carriage please." She was glad only Mr. and Mrs. Carter were present. "I would rather you not mention—"

"Call Lady Edgemont a public carriage. She won't want to take one from the house," the housekeeper said. "Jean, come with me. We'll put a basket together for you both."

Mr. Carter took her portmanteau and showed her to a seat by the hearth.

With the decision made, Patrice was eager to be on her way. Every moment she remained was painful.

Jean and Mrs. Carter returned with a basket.

"There is some reading material for you," Mrs. Carter said.

Patrice lifted the cloth on top of the basket and found a stack of letters tied with string. All of them were addressed to her. Patrice gave the housekeeper a questioning stare.

"Lady Montgomery requested that all calling cards and letters sent to you be held while you were in mourning." The housekeeper eyed her husband. "Except those from Mrs. Bainbridge and your friends."

"It is most fortunate that I am no longer in mourning." Patrice replaced the cloth over the basket.

"I didn't like keeping them from you," the housekeeper muttered.

"Thank you, Mrs. Carter."

"The carriage is waiting for you in the alley." The butler picked up her portmanteau.

"That won't be necessary, Mr. Carter. You both have done enough. I don't want to get anyone else involved." She thanked the couple and with Jean, left through the servant entrance. She wasn't a coward, but she didn't want a scene and more gossip, and if she were honest, she didn't want to see her parents or Mr. Armstrong.

On the second day of their trip, she looked at the calling cards and letters that had been sent to her. She read each one. Some were from people who were unknown to her. She assumed they were from Edgemont's business acquaintances. Others were from her friends in Sommer-by-the-Sea, her mother's friends, Count and Countess Pushchin. There was a second bundle of messages from more friends, a priest from Russia, Prussian Prince Gebhard von Blucher, and the Grand Duke of the House of Breuce.

The rest of the four-day ride was a blur. That part of her life was over.

Roused from her musing, Patrice gave herself a shake and looked at her friends around the table. "At last, I'm home. I mourned Edgemont. I even set his business on its proper course and kept it out of money hungry hands. The Edgemont line died with him. The book is closed, not only on that part of my life, and the part with George Armstrong, but on all men. To be blunt, they can all go to the devil."

# CHAPTER TWO

"I UNDERSTAND. EDGEMONT'S death was an unexpected blow. And George was a scoundrel. But you will heal. You may still find love. Not all men are—"

"Opportunistic? Worthless?" Patrice interrupted Tanya. "I meant what I said. They can all—"

"There's no need for you to say it again. You made your point." Tanya studied her for several minutes. The proprietress reached over and took Patrice's teacup and looked at the dredges. The twinkle in her eyes morphed into a solemn expression.

Inwardly, Patrice moaned. Tanya was serious about her tea reading, but she didn't want to encourage her friend. Instead, Patrice put her hand on her arm.

"I love you dearly, but I am not good company."

"You try too hard to make that evident. Humor me. I listened to your poems. The least you can do is let me play my game.

"Pick up the cup with your left hand and silently ask your question. When you're done, swirl the cup three times counter-clockwise, cover the cup with the saucer, then turn them upside down."

Patrice sighed. A few more minutes with Tanya wouldn't hurt. Perhaps a diversion would help her mood. A little laughter would be good.

Love wasn't part of the equation in a marriage, at least the emotional part wasn't. If anything, marriage was all posturing and calculating. What family to attract? What to offer? What to bargain? What to settle on? Emotion and love weren't an option, not really. Marriage was strictly a business game of transactions.

She did everything according to the requirements of her social position—married the right man, who had the right business acumen, the right family. According to her mother, her long friendship with Edgemont was sufficient, better than most girls could expect and love, love found people over time. It found Edgemont…with someone else.

Then the debacle that was Armstrong. At least by standing up for herself, she was able to avoid that disaster. Which led to one conclusion. The only person who knew what was best for Patrice Montgomery Edgemont *was* Patrice Montgomery Edgemont.

Perhaps Edgemont's last gift to her was the greatest of all. As a widow she was free of society's scrutiny and men controlling every aspect of her life. For that, she was thankful.

She reveled at the thought of being free and let out a long sigh of contentment. It was time for her to take control, do what she wanted, follow her heart.

Heart. Did she have one? It didn't beat with excitement or anticipation. These days, she raised her heart rate wading through business papers Mr. Lacey sent for her review.

Patrice stared at the small pool of liquid and twigs in the bottom of her teacup. Her question?

*Coward.* She didn't have the nerve to ask, nor did she want to hear the answer. She didn't need a third loss. She didn't know if she would be able to recover.

No. Never again. Her life was fine. She was fine. No longer would she assume the part of the victim.

The heroine. That's the role she wanted.

Patrice picked up the cup with her left hand. Her question? Where would her new-found freedom take her?

With a counterclockwise motion, she swirled her cup three times, then inverted it over her saucer. After a minute, Patrice turned the cup upright and handed it to Tanya who studied the pattern the leaves made.

"Notice how the tea leaves scatter in the bowl. There is meaning to where they land. The rim is the present, the side shows events close at hand, and the bottom is the distant future."

Patrice studied the leaves along with Tanya. She soon gave up. Where Tanya discovered prophecy, she found sludge.

"The tea leaves form pictures. Overall, your leaves reveal good fortune. The anchor, palm tree, and triangles." Tanya pointed to the dregs in her cup. "The anchor means success in business or in love."

"Yes. My solicitor congratulated me. I walked away from an almost disastrous marriage to Armstrong and saved the Edgemont business. I would say I was successful on both counts." She may have sounded caustic, but it was the truth.

"Don't be so sarcastic," Tanya snapped, although a smile smudged her lips. "Palm trees are a positive omen, also success—in anything you do. For single people it means marriage."

Patrice leaned over to examine the inside of the cup. Tanya pulled it away.

"You know you're not allowed to see the leaves." She returned to the cup. "Triangles indicate a boon of some kind." Tanya tilted the cup. "Ah, heart shapes—a lover, and much success."

Patrice waited, her patience running thin, as Tanya studied the teacup for several minutes.

"I've never seen a grouping of leaves like this. They keep pointing to marriage."

"Oh, no. I told you, I. Am. Through. With. Men."

Tanya ignored her and kept studying the delicate china cup. "It looks like an 'H.' It represents the first letter of *his* name. There is also an indication that he is tall, with dark hair, and is handsome by every woman's standard."

"I'm greatly relieved. My mystery man is definitely not Armstrong."

"The image of the letter sits near the rim. You'll find out soon." Tanya sat back.

"Is that all?" Patrice asked.

Tanya focused on the tea leaves, tipped the cup in another direction. "Reading the tea leaves is an art rather than a science. Your leaves are much like you, no hidden meanings," she raised her eyes and glanced at Patrice, "and at times difficult. This reading is not simple." Patrice bent closer for a view.

"The swan has several meanings. My first impression is two people, relationship, but with six dots surrounding it I don't think this represents love." Tanya glanced at her.

"Children? God's little toe, no, not that."

Tanya raised an eyebrow and gave her a look that did not disguise her annoyance. "No. Not children."

"That's a relief. Six children are a bit much to bear." Patrice struggled to contain a playful smile.

"The swan represents a pair, a couple, perhaps this is the number two. Two plus six, eight. Does that number mean anything to you?" Patrice shook her head. "No? The swan can also signify good luck. Perhaps in six days, six weeks."

"For me, probably six years."

Tanya glared at her and returned to the cup. "There also appears to be an aura of crisis closing in on you, and danger. Daggers are never a good sign, especially at the bottom of the cup. These are unique. Long lines underneath indicate a journey."

"A dangerous journey?"

"And they point toward the handle." Tanya straightened in her chair quickly, so quickly she almost bumped her head into Patrice's. When she looked up, a shadow of alarm touched Tanya's face. "You need to go home. Now."

"I didn't need you to read the leaves to tell me that." Patrice stood and pointed toward the cup. "Please, let me take a look at the leaves before I leave."

She took the cup from Tanya and studied it closely, tilting it from one side to the other.

"Just as I suspected. I see hot mushroom barley soup, bread, a nice cup of tea, and a warm fire in my very near future."

"As a matter of fact, I agree with you." She turned to the table behind her, retrieved the parcel. "I know how much you like the soup." Tanya handed it to Patrice.

Patrice took a deep breath. The aroma of the hearty soup brought a smile to her lips.

"I do not like this weather." Tanya glanced out the window. "It reminds me of St. Petersburg. Snow like this can be deadly." She turned to Patrice her brows crunched together. "Snow is in your future; lots of snow. Are you going to the lodge?"

"I was told it's been snowing for a week." Patrice thought nothing of her comment.

"Yes, yes, but I mean a blizzard. Are you going to the lodge?"

"No. I'm not staying at The Mooring. I'm staying with Anna." The urgency in Tanya's voice had her concerned. "Why? Did you see that in my future, too?"

"Nothing. Be careful. That's all." She turned to the ladies. "I must get back to the kitchen. Thank you for my Valentine."

"Before you go, where did you learn to read tea leaves?" Effie sat with her elbow on the table, her chin in her hand. "I find it fascinating."

Tanya gave her a mysterious glare. "One doesn't learn to read the leaves. You are chosen, given the gift. I've read the leaves ever since I was a child."

"You're not a Romani woman," Anna said.

"No. I am not. But I do wonder why I enjoy the balalaika and reading tea leaves." Tanya accentuated her almost non-existent Russian accent.

A cold gust of air burst into the room as the door to the shop opened. Swirls of snow preceded Lord Barrington and Magistrate Rogers as they entered. They brushed the snow off their greatcoats. They glanced at the dining area and made their way to Tanya.

"Good afternoon, ladies." Lord Barrington touched the brim

of his hat. "Mrs. Chernokov, a moment, if I may."

"Of course. This way, please." Lord Barrington and Tanya stepped to the side.

"I've requested Lord Barrington's assistance." Magistrate Rogers stood uncomfortably by the table. "It appears Lord Lieutenant Hugh Percy's son has gone missing."

The ladies exchanged glances, their faces filled with concern.

"When was the boy last seen?" Anna looked at the other ladies.

"I had no idea Lord Percy was in the village." Effie hardly waited for Anna to finish her question.

"What was the boy doing out in this weather? Was he alone?" Hattie spoke over the chatter of the others.

"Ladies, ladies, one at a time. He's missing and there are..." Rogers hesitated when he noticed Barrington had rejoined them, "foreigners and vagrants by the woods. The same area where young Henry was last seen."

"Yes, Rogers. Others were seen there, too." Barrington cast a disapproving glance at the man before he turned to Tanya.

"Forgive—"

"There is nothing to forgive. I have come across intolerance. I appreciate that you are with the magistrate."

Barrington gave her a gracious nod and continued. "There has also been a sighting of a wild boar. The men have scoured the woods on the cliff and moved north, well past the houses in that area. We are concerned since Percy is visiting and not familiar with our woods. The young lad is inquisitive and a bit reckless. We had people search the caves along the coast and fortunately they didn't find him there. As the weather worsens, his family's worries increase."

"Lord Barrington, if I may?"

He turned to Patrice.

"What was Lord Percy's boy doing out in this weather?"

"He was running errands for his older brother, delivering Valentine's greetings to several ladies, and is overdue at home.

We're speaking to every shop owner and searching every house and building in the area, especially along the cliff where he was last seen. The weather is getting worse, and there is concern for his welfare. My friends and I are helping the magistrate since his men are on assignment at Bamburgh Castle. Once we're finished here, we're off to the woods."

"Let me help. I'll search my hunting lodge." Patrice noticed Tanya raise her eyebrows. She felt like sticking out her tongue at the woman. "It will be one less place for you to search. If young Percy was in the woods, he may have gone there to get out of the weather."

"That won't be necessary. We will be there shortly. This is not the weather for you to go traipsing in the woods."

"Nonsense. I am more than capable. I've been locked up so long a small adventure would be welcome."

"I would bring you to The Mooring myself, but I must speak to Lord Percy. If you could wait?"

"No, no. You meet with Lord Percy. I'll check the house and lodge and give you a full report when you arrive. Hopefully, I can hand over young Henry safe and sound." Barrington's concern touched her, but it was unnecessary.

"You have my thanks. The quicker we find the boy the better, especially with all the signs pointing to this storm worsening," Barrington said.

"If I may, Lady Edgemont." Rogers drew Patrice's attention. "Have you been back to The Mooring?"

"Not yet, why do you ask?"

"I've kept watch on the estate as you asked, and noticed some of the larger trees have come down. The house and lodge have not been affected, but the fallen trees have diverted the stream and caused boggy areas and pools of water where you wouldn't expect them. Be careful when you're in the woods. As cold as it is, the shallow water is all ice and now covered with snow."

"Rogers is quite correct. You really shouldn't go traipsing in the snow alone." Barrington's concerned look touched a memory.

"Barrington, that is the same glare you gave me when we were younger."

"And you were reckless." From the light in his eyes, he remembered those days, too.

"Magistrate." She turned to Rogers. "I'm familiar with the grounds, woods, even the stream. I assure you I'll be fine. For all we know young Percy is skating on the frozen lake."

Barrington chuckled. "If I remember correctly, you cheered on my friends and me when we had skating races on the lake. I also remember lingering behind and racing with you. Please. Be careful. This storm is treacherous and deceptive."

Patrice's icy veneer softened. If there was anyone she could trust, it was Reese Barrington. His concern was genuine and, if she admitted it, greatly appreciated.

"I'll come by The Mooring as soon as I can." He turned to the women. "Ladies, if you will excuse us. Come, Rogers, we have much to do."

Barrington nodded and left with the magistrate in tow.

"Anna, I must go home." Patrice watched the backs of the men leave the shop.

"Yes, I agree. Take my carriage. Hattie will get me home. My coachman can help you search the lodge then bring you back."

"Thank you, but I'd rather remain at home in case the boy wanders by."

"Are you sure? Should I send Jean? Your staff hasn't returned."

"No need. I'll be fine. And thank you for your carriage. I'll send your man back quickly." Patrice got up and gathered her things, said her good-byes, and made her way to the door.

"Don't forget your Valentine's gift." Tanya handed her the bundle.

"Never. After traipsing the woods, your soup will be in order. It brings back memories of my time in St. Petersburg last year. It was snowing then, too."

"It always snows in St. Petersburg." Amusement flickered in Tanya's eyes.

Patrice squeezed her hand and left the shop. She made her way to Anna's carriage through a heavy snowfall which was more intent than when she arrived.

One breath and the deep, bone-chilling cold made it difficult to breathe. The snow was halfway up the carriage wheels. Without wasting time, she stepped into the carriage. The coachman placed a blanket across her lap. She snuggled down to keep warm for the short ride to The Mooring.

The carriage pulled away. The ground was a patchwork of ice and mud. The gray sky showed no signs of the snow letting up. Perhaps Tanya was right about a blizzard. It didn't appear the snowfall would stop any time soon.

The carriage plodded along Castle Hill Road and turned onto High Cliff Road. After several minutes, they made their way down The Mooring's drive. The expanse from the road to the house looked pristine, the snow marked only by occasional animal tracks.

As they came over the rise, she stared at the lifeless house, a dark silhouette against the gray sky and curtain of snow. She had only driven past the house last November, and hadn't been inside in ten months. It wasn't until now that she realized how much she missed being here. It confirmed what she already knew. She never should have left.

The carriage pulled up under the front portico. The coachman came down and opened the carriage door.

"Lady Edgemont, your key if I may." He held out his hand.

She opened her reticule, found the key on a silk string with a tassel, and handed it to the man.

"Please wait here while I inspect the house."

"That won't be necessary." She pulled the rug off her lap and slid forward.

"Please, Lady Edgemont. I won't be but a few minutes."

She was about to tell him again it wasn't necessary, but a

small shiver of apprehension told her there was no harm in him looking about.

"Very well." She moved back but left the rug discarded.

She watched him unlock the door and pass inside. Moments later candlelight progressed from one room to the other.

All her life she wanted an adventure. She thought she would have it with Edgemont. When he was gone, possibly an adventure with Armstrong. But it was invigorating, more wonderful and fearful when she realized she could have an adventure on her own terms. No rules and no one to answer to. The *ton* be damned.

It took the coachman more than a few minutes. All in all, it was an hour before he returned. He came outside and opened the carriage door to hand her down.

"Everything is in good order." He brought her inside.

She stood in the entranceway looking at the grand staircase and was suddenly anxious. Everything around her was both familiar and unfamiliar at the same time.

The coachman held the candle and ushered her to the main level. From where she stood she could see light coming from the parlor. Gravitating toward the welcoming glow, she entered the room and found a fire in the grate and the dust covers off the furniture, folded, and stacked in a neat pile.

"Excellent." The room was barely warm. There were cobwebs in the corners and dust covered the wood floor. Nothing she couldn't take care of. "You have outdone yourself."

"It will take some time to heat the room. If you tell me where to find a blanket I will fetch it for you." The concerned expression on the coachman's face confused her. "Begging your pardon, Lady Edgemont, I can bring you to Lady Marianna. The weather does not look good." He took a breath. "I didn't mean to speak out of turn."

"I appreciate your concern. The weather *is* getting worse. You best be on your way. Please give my thanks to Lady Marianna."

He still looked anxious when he left. She listened to the tapping of his feet down the marble stairs. The front door closed with a finality she hadn't experienced before.

Patrice stared out the window as the man hauled himself onto the carriage, grabbed the reins, and drove away. The snow was almost three-quarters of the way up the wheel.

The house was silently still as though it were asleep and hadn't woken. The only sounds were the snap of the fire in the hearth and her pounding heart. Patrice hadn't moved from the window as she focused on the woods. They looked foreboding in the waning daylight. There was no sense in procrastinating. The sooner she went to the lodge, the sooner she could be back in front of the warm fire.

Her decision made, she hurried up the stairs and into her room to change into something more fitting for a trek in the snow. Her furniture was draped, and the bed stripped of its linens. There was plenty of time to take care of that later.

She hurried across the room and rummaged in the bottom of her closet for the old trousers and shirt she wore when she plodded around the estate. Both were gifts from Mrs. Bainbridge. It would feel good to get out of her dress.

From her bedroom window she usually had a good view of the garden with its large maze, the forest beyond the garden wall, and not far from the cliff's edge, the roof of the hunting lodge. She clearly saw the outline of the garden maze, the first structure Edgemont added when he took ownership of the house. To him it was a game, to her, an adventure.

On the other side of the garden wall, she barely made out the forest and saw nothing of the lodge. She went back to her closet and found a pair of heavy wool gloves. As an afterthought, she took her red wool cap.

Dressed and ready, she pinned up her hair, put on her cap, and went down the service stairs to the kitchen. The room was almost warm. The coachman had started the stove. Her bundle from Tanya was on the table.

She found what she needed on a hook by the garden door, and shrugged into her husband's old hunting jacket and tugged on her garden boots. As an afterthought, she grabbed a few things she thought she might need if Henry was indeed at the lodge. She quickly stuffed them into the jacket pockets, along with some tea and scones. The boy might be hungry.

She opened the kitchen door and could barely make out the garden gate in the back wall. Adjusting her cap, she pulled on her gloves. The snow was marred with the single set of tracks, a rabbit's, she guessed. She pulled a walking stick from its place by the door. She was ready.

"Adventure, here I come."

# CHAPTER THREE

NIKOLAI BARANOV SAID good-bye to Tatiana and left the tearoom. He wasn't sure if he was proud or crushed. Lady Edgemont walked past him, looked him in the eyes, and from her vacant stare, had no idea who he was.

She was supposed to be in London. It was why he took on this task rather than sent someone else. Now, with things in motion, there was nothing he could do but see it through.

He headed toward the docks in the village harbor. It was the best place to stay out of sight. He sat by himself in the Anchor Inn with a tankard of ale passing time until his meeting. His mind was on another winter, another mission, another disaster.

War had taught him many lessons, but it hadn't prepared him for the manipulation and maneuvering that ran rampant in politics. His father, however, thrived on the challenges.

Grand Duke Anton Stephanovich Baranov of the House of Breuce was a master at diplomacy, diversion, and duplicity all in the name of Tzar Alexander I. Nikolai's espionage expertise was a talent his father counted on in his business.

Until last year, Nikolai had been doing a good job of working exclusively for the Tzar –only working with his father when the Tzar deemed it necessary. He remembered the last event all too clearly.

"Nikolai, wake up." Someone shook him gently. "Nikolai.

I've been pounding on your door." Startled, he blinked to focus his eyes.

He had been dreaming of riding, enjoying the freedom and open air. His dream faded as his head cleared. Gone was the grassy steppe and his muscular horse beneath him. His racing heart began to quiet. Another glance. His mother stood at his side.

He sprang up on his elbows.

"What is it?" His mother hadn't ventured into his room since he was a boy. Fully awake, he grabbed for his robe.

"Your father sent word. You're to meet him at Count Pushchin's residence."

His mother went to his closet and pulled out his clothes.

"Where's Gleb?"

"I wasn't about to wake the entire household staff."

Gleb was more than a valet. Nikolai rang for him as he went to his mother's side.

"You haven't got time—"

"Mother. Go downstairs."

His valet quietly entered.

"If I may, Lady Baranov?" The valet held out his hands gesturing toward the clothes she held.

"Give the clothes to Gleb and go downstairs. I will be with you as soon as I dress." He walked his mother into the hallway then gently urged her on. Once she started off, he returned to his room and closed the door.

"But Nikolai," she said through the closed door.

"As soon as I am dressed. See if there is any coffee."

"I can get you—" Gleb's voice had an indignant ring to it.

"That's not necessary." He looked at the door and listened to his mother's retreating footsteps. "She needed something to do, that's all."

He turned to the valet. He had returned the clothes his mother had chosen and brought him something more appropriate. That made him stop. Appropriate for what?

"Gleb, what do you know." His valet was always a source of information. Nikolai was already out of his bedclothes and at his washstand.

"Someone entered Count Pushchin's residence, unannounced."

Nikolai stopped his ministrations and looked in the mirror focused on his man. "Unannounced. That's no cause to call out the militia." He returned his focus to the task at hand and waited for more information.

"Apparently rather than use a door, he came through a window, on the second floor."

He froze as his heart began to pound. "What else?" he asked without looking up.

"Items belonging to Lady Edgemont were taken while she slept." Nikolai's head sprang up.

A chill ran down his spine, the hairs stood at attention up his arms. He could sense there was more.

"Was she—" Alarm and anger rippled up his spine.

"No. She was not harmed."

Nikolai grabbed the towel from Gleb's hand and hurried into his clothes.

"Have my horse ready at once," he said as his valet helped him into his coat.

He hurried down the stairs to his mother before Gleb had a chance to respond.

"Where's Father?" He looked around the parlor as his mother handed him his coffee. She was the only one in the room.

"A messenger from your father arrived a short time ago. He's with Count Pushchin and Lord Edgemont."

The coffee was hot and strong. He finished it quickly and put on his greatcoat and hat.

"His message was short and clear. He didn't give me any details, just tell you to come to the villa at once."

He started for the door.

"Nikolai."

He faced her and saw a sadness he had seen before, when he left to defend Moscow against the French invaders two years ago.

He went to her and kissed her forehead and was surprised when she put her arms around him and held him tight.

"Mother, what is it?" He held her away and looked into her eyes.

The soft patter of feet on the staircase made him look up. His sister Anya was at the door.

"Leonid told me that all is not well with Father's business. Changes are going to have to be made. You can no longer be at arm's length," Anya said. "None of us can."

He didn't say anything, just gave her a curt nod, kissed his mother, and went out the door.

In a matter of minutes, Nikolai was in front of the villa and was shown into the count's library.

His father stood at the mantel, his eyes unblinking, focused on the floor. Leonid was by the trolley pouring himself some vodka. The count was at the hearth, feeding papers into the fire. He looked around the room. No one else was there.

"It's a bit early for vodka, even for you," he said to his brother-in-law.

"Good, you're here." His father gestured for him to sit down. "We have some things to work out quickly."

"Where are the count's guests?" Nikolai asked.

"That's why I had you come here. There is an unease in the city. This attack is an omen of what's to come. I've a message from Tzar Alexander. For Lady Edgemont's safety, she will be joining the British Ambassador's entourage. We are fortunate that he is leaving today to return to London. The count and countess will be Lady Edgemont's escort."

The fire flared as the last of the papers were tossed in.

"No disrespect." He faced his father. "But I don't think the count or the countess would be any help if there was trouble." His patience was wearing thin.

"You think you're better suited," the count said a smirk on his face. "Do you want to ruin her? A young handsome man escorting a married woman in place of her husband would start tongues wagging and bring attention to her."

"And to their trip to Russia?" Nikolai asked.

"That's enough." His father moved between them. "I don't think she is in any danger. The ambassador is traveling on a British navy vessel."

"You are right. Everyone's tensions are high with the robbery." The count turned to Nikolai brushing imaginary dust from his hands. "I know you mean well. You have a job to do as I have mine."

"Nikolai, you have a more pressing challenge. Edgemont is needed at a meeting in four weeks. Rather than risk him traveling to London and back, he is staying in St. Petersburg. To keep him safe, our friends at the Church of St. Catherine have offered him shelter. To the outside world, you and he will be young men seeking to become brothers at the church. Guard him well. Neither the Tzar nor I trust anyone else."

Nikolai hadn't stopped staring at the count.

"Tell me what was stolen." He had gone with Lord and Lady Edgemont to the ballet and out to dinner the night before. Lord Edgemont was called to a high-ranking meeting in the middle of the ballet, so Nikolai had escorted Lady Edgemont the rest of the evening.

"It's none of your concern," the count said, dismissing his question with a wave of his hand.

The count was frightened. That was obvious. That didn't excuse his behavior. Nikolai, the son of a grand duke, was a prince of the realm and commanded more respect. Instead of calling the man out, it took all his effort to hold back. His father stood next to him and put his arm around his shoulders to calm him.

"Pushchin doesn't like his house invaded." The two older men exchanged glances. The tension in the room went down several degrees.

"Come, with me." On his way out with his father, they spoke with Leonid. "Stay with Edgemont. He wants to take his wife to the ship. Once you're done there, take him to St. Catherine's and wait with him until Nikolai arrives. I want Edgemont taken to safety as soon as possible."

Nikolai and his father went up the grand staircase. "The countess gave Lady Edgemont the last room on this hallway. It has a balcony and fine view of the garden."

"And obviously easy access." Nikolai held back a moan.

They entered the now empty room. The closet doors stood open. Only a few hangers were apparent. The bed linens were tossed. The dresser drawers were open and empty.

"This is the count's handiwork. When Edgemont saw what he had done he was furious. Anything that could have helped us determine who did this was destroyed." His father looked around in disgust.

"And you still have him, and the countess, escorting Lady Edgemont to England?"

"With the English Navy and the British ambassador. She will be safe."

Nikolai looked at the doors that led to the balcony. The latch had been replaced with a simple hook and eye. He examined the outside of the door and found scratches that indicated something may have been put under the engaged hook and forced it up.

He went to the edge of the balcony and looked over the side. The ground was a sheer three stories below. The side of the house was covered with creeping vines.

"I examined the trellis before you arrived. Several pieces of wood have been recently damaged. I suspect whoever entered, used the trellis as a ladder, unlocked the door, and entered."

"Where is Lady Edgemont?" An uncomfortable feeling was screaming at him.

"She is with the countess preparing to leave."

Nikolai turned to his father. "What was stolen?"

"Nothing was disturbed except the drawer that held Lady

Edgemont's jewelry."

"The thief knew where to look," he said.

His father nodded. "All her jewels were taken."

"Don't tell me. Edgemont put the Royal Brooch with his wife's jewelry."

His father nodded.

"Why am I not surprised? He would think of it as a game. Find the precious gem among the others."

"The thieves didn't have to guess. All the jewels, including the brooch, were taken." His father led him from the room back to the library.

"Who knows its significance other than the Tzar, Edgemont, you, and me?"

"I would swear no one. Not even the count. Although this theft would prove me wrong." The circles under his father's eyes concerned him. He had never seen him this worried.

"We may be going down a false trail. The thief may have simply been after Lady Edgemont's jewels and knew nothing about the brooch." Nikolai knew at once his father didn't agree when he saw his pained, watery stare.

"If the thieves took the brooch intentionally, they still need the document that goes with it. It's one of Edgemont's games. Only he knows how to solve the puzzle."

"You may be right, but we cannot take that chance." His father restlessly paced the room as he spoke to him. "Edgemont was astonished when Alexander offered the brooch. *'To show his good faith.'* That's what the Tzar told me."

"I was with the Tzar when Edgemont asked for a unique key, something someone would surrender to the keeper of the document as identification." Nikolai didn't know why Edgemont didn't use a secret word. He wouldn't consider it. He wanted an object. "Your brother-in-law offered the brooch. It's over three hundred years old, and only a handful of people have ever seen it. It fit Edgemont's criteria."

"Edgemont told me this morning he had no idea what to do

with it other than put it with his wife's jewels." His father uncharacteristically ran his hand through his hair. "He said she was asleep when he went to her room. He put the brooch into the jewel case and instead of leaving it out as he found it, he tucked it away with her clothes.

"In the morning he was concerned she would think the case was taken and went to tell her. That's when he found her asleep and the jewel case open and empty."

His father went over to the trolley and glanced at him over his shoulder. "Would you like…" he gestured to the coffee and liquor.

"No, no, but you go ahead."

His father nodded and poured a cup of coffee for himself.

"I want you to stay with Edgemont until the meeting. Once that is done, you will get him back to England." His father sipped the coffee and put down the cup. "I'll be happy when this is over. Now, go. Gleb will bring you what you need."

Nikolai looked at his father. He had seen worry in the man's eyes before, but for the first time he saw doubt.

"You are right." His father looked at him. "Someone close had to be involved. I've always known who is with me and who is not. This… This is different. It's not one person. Who do I trust?"

"We may not always agree, but I am with you."

Grand Duke Anton Stephanovich Baranov looked at his son. The doubt of moments ago turned to pride.

His father took his face in both his hands and kissed him. He held him at arm's length and stared for several minutes.

Nikolai hoped he saw a proud son, one who loved him.

"I've gotten you involved in something I cannot control. *Bud' ostorozhen, moy lev.*"

Be careful, my lion.

FOR THE NEXT four weeks, he and Edgemont remained in the church. They were constant companions. He found the Englishman easy to talk to and be with. Their political discussions were at times heated. Their views concerning art and music were similar. But when it came to family, their devotion was the same. Nonetheless, the reason for their isolation was a cloud that hung over them. They were baffled by the robbery. They knew someone they trusted had betrayed them, and for what? Political advancement? Financial gain? Family rivalry?

They were also aware that the brooch meant nothing without the document. As often as Nikolai tried to encourage Edgemont to tell him what the document contained and who had it, the man refused. Wait until the meeting, he'd say. Wait until the meeting.

The two became close friends. By the end of the adventure, Nikolai was sure the secret would be safe, he and Edgemont would part ways, and he would never see Lady Edgemont again.

Yet there she was. It was Benedict Edgemont who was gone forever.

"Another ale?"

Nikolai, stirred from his musings, looked at the barmaid with a pitcher of ale in her hand.

St. Petersburg faded, replaced by the noise and drinking at the Anchor Inn.

He put his hand over his tankard. The woman moved on.

Nikolai finished his ale and left the tavern. It was time for his appointment.

# CHAPTER FOUR

WELL-HIDDEN IN THE moonless night, Nikolai turned down Knight's Lane. Since Edgemont's death, he had been investigating the theft of the brooch, following every piece of information, speaking to whomever had evidence, anything that would bring him closer to finding the gem. There was a great deal at stake. A recent fact came to light and needed to be confirmed. Someone needed to speak to the contact. It meant going to Sommer-by-the-Sea.

He volunteered. Once he had the details he would leave, and no one would be any wiser.

He hurried to Number 21 and knocked on Donald Philby's door.

"Come."

He entered. The single candle burning did little to light the room and instead gave it a clandestine feeling. The curtains were drawn making the small room almost as dark inside as outside.

Philby, in a crisp white shirt, lifted his head and stared at him as if he'd seen a ghost.

"I'm glad to see you, too." Nikolai closed the door behind him.

"I didn't expect you. I thought they would send someone else, not you." Philby slowly got to his feet. "I wish you had stayed in the homeland."

"I was careful. You said you had information."

He didn't miss Philby's pained expression. Something was out of place. The voice in the back of his head screamed it was a trap. He glanced at Philby.

Bloody hell. The man wasn't afraid of being discovered. He had already been exposed. Philby was the bait.

Nikolai pulled his knife. He heard more than saw the door open. A gust of wind blew out the candle, throwing the room into total darkness.

He wasn't far from the door. Half-a-dozen paces at most. *Move.* He was halfway to his goal when he sensed someone to his right. Philby? A jab to his stomach knocked the breath out of him.

Doubled over, Nikolai turned his head and focused on the shuffling sounds behind him while he breathed slowly to get control of his lungs and racing heart. There was no getting away from the inevitable. He had been in brawls before. In his current state, this was not going to go well.

Out of nowhere, something hit him from behind. Hot pain shot down his neck and back. He turned to face the attacker, but he was unsteady.

He staggered, trying to stay upright, but he had difficulty getting his feet to work. He raised his arms to protect himself and blinked trying to clear his vision.

*Concentrate before you get yourself killed. You must be close to who stole the gem for them to take this action now.*

He heard more than saw the scuffle on the other side of the room.

*Don't think about Philby. He's on his own. Get yourself out of here. Now.*

The flash of a blade and searing pain had him on his knees. His knife dropped from his hand and skidded across the floor. He attempted to shake his head demanding it to clear. Instead, he keeled over.

His head throbbed and his middle ached as he struggled to gain some control of his senses. Someone pulled him by his collar.

It wasn't difficult for him to pretend he was dead.

"What have you done, you idiot? Alive. We needed them both alive."

In his current state, the voice was too muffled for him to identify.

"Don't leave anything behind. Can you do that, or must I do it myself?"

Nikolai's head throbbed more than his stomach hurt. He kept his eyes closed and didn't move. Just a few more minutes and his head would clear. He took a deep breath.

*That's it. Another.*

Fish? Whale oil? He sniffed the air. *Fire*, was his last thought before he passed out.

A muffled voice reached him through the cobwebs. "Baranov. Baranov." The voice was strident and urgent. He took a breath and began to cough. That's when he heard the pounding on the door. Another breath and the coughing got worse.

His eyes flew open. Smoke filled the room. There were flames all around him. He had no idea how long he'd been out. Ignoring the pain in his stomach and the blood seeping from the cut, he tried to move as quickly and quietly as possible.

"Mr. Philby. Are you there?" someone said on the other side of the door. "Break the door down before this fire sets all the houses in flames."

"Nikolai, thank god." Philby, who had been bending over him, fell back against his desk. "Leave. Now. While you can. Go. And don't trust anyone."

Shaking himself into action, he stood and tried to pull Philby to his feet. The man raised his head. That's when Nikolai saw Philby's shirt. The front covered in blood.

"I'll get you out of here." Nikolai bent down to lift him. Philby pushed him away with his last bit of strength.

"Where am I going? They know who I am. Listen to me. You're the only one left. Find out who is responsible." Philby tried to lift his head. "Don't trust anyone. Do you hear, no one."

"Let me help you up." Nikolai reached to pull Philby up.

Philby swatted his hand away. "In the closet, there's a panel. The tunnel behind it will take you two streets away. They have no idea you are in England." He chuckled and began to cough. "They think you're a vagrant. Take my hat and coat. Do you hear me? My hat and coat. You must take it. They won't recognize you as the man who came in here."

He heard someone breaking down the door.

"Go. Now. Don't trust anyone." Philby's voice was so low he could barely hear. "Go."

Nikolai snatched Philby's hat and coat off the rack.

"I'm almost through." It was the magistrate's voice.

Nikolai stepped into the closet and closed the door as he heard people enter the room.

"Over here. It's Mr. Philby. Get him out," came the muffled voices on the other side of the closet. "Are you sure you saw someone else come here?"

Nikolai felt along the walls. Nothing except a molding that split the wall in half. He thought Philby may have been daft, until his hand felt the small latch embedded in the wood trim.

Relieved, he sprang the mechanism. The half door swung open. He stepped into the tunnel and closed the door behind him.

The space was cramped as he sweated and hurried along listening for sounds of someone following him, waiting for someone to try and stop him.

A cold breeze rushed across his face. He was close to the end of the tunnel. He'd have to be careful because he had no idea where he would wind up. The tunnel turned and he came face to face with an iron gate. Crates and barrels were stacked on the other side.

Nikolai tried the old rusty latch. To his surprise, it was well oiled. He had to admire Philby: his friend kept the escape route operational. He slipped into Philby's hat and coat, shimmied through the small space, and past the obstruction.

Ridding himself of his vagabond gait, he walked down the

main street as if he owned one of the big mansions along the cliff.

People rushed past him to the fire. He continued on Knight's Lane as if he belonged there, on his way out of Sommer-by-the-Sea.

# CHAPTER FIVE

THE WIND WHIPPED around, making it difficult for Patrice to see as she trudged in knee-deep snow across the field toward the woods. The more she thought about the possibility of young Henry being at the lodge, the more ridiculous the idea seemed. But she gave Barrington her word and like it or not, she kept on going.

How foolish and utterly unthinking she had been after Edgemont died. Her mother said she needed to do some soul searching, understand and resolve her issues with the dearly departed, forgive him. Staying by herself would be too difficult, her mother insisted. She would be better taken care of at Montgomery Hall, not her own London home. Her mother's small staff could hardly handle the hall, let alone a house guest.

She spoke with Mr. Peters, Edgemont's solicitor, about hiring Bow Street Runners to investigate Edgemont's murder. While she discussed the matter with him, her brother was murdered. Her parents forbade her to take any action. It would only bring her more grief. What good would it serve? Her name was on everyone's lips. Her family was already in ruin.

So, she stayed at her parents' home with brief visits to her own Edgemont Arms. But worst of all, instead of standing up for herself she regressed into a non-thinking fool.

And Edgemont. She did do a bit of soul searching and found

that the hopes and dreams Edgemont painted for them were nothing more than empty, meaningless words. She never expected to be the center of his universe. God's middle toe, no. They were individuals, but he gave her no indication that she would be inconsequential. There were times he couldn't get away from her fast enough. Even on their trip to St Petersburg. The mere mention he was needed, and he left her with their escort.

Edgemont had been attentive, witty, and thoughtful when their friendship turned to courting. He traveled for business, yet always made time for her. But several months after their marriage, something changed. There was no event, no day, nothing monumental. It just happened.

How excited she was when he surprised her with the deed to The Mooring. It had been her summer home since she was a child and a place where she, Brian, and Edgemont explored. As they got older, she remained friends with Edgemont. They often walked the cliff and enjoyed the sea air.

Now she understood his eagerness to buy her The Mooring. It served two purposes. Her father needed money. At least the house would stay in the family. More importantly to Edgemont, it was his way of banishing her to the country. In the twenty-four months they were married, she spent eighteen of them alone, mostly in Sommer-by-the-Sea.

When he was with her, there was always someone he needed to meet, someplace he needed to be. Anyone, anyplace was better than being with her.

Then there was the manner of her husband's death. Edgemont wasn't a rake. A mistress. How could she not know he had one? She saw it so easily with others in the *ton*.

Rehashing this over and over didn't make the pain any less. Was it really pain, or if she were truthful, was it her pride that was crushed?

How naïve she had been. How clever Edgemont was. Her family name, connections, and prestige were a sought-after commodity. It drove Edgemont, and Armstrong as well.

She stabbed the ground with her walking stick and stomped on through the snow, annoyed for allowing herself to wallow in self-pity. All these months she had kept it bottled up.

She wanted to exorcise both men from her mind, from everything, and put it all behind her. She had already started to claim her independence when she and Jean left London. Why was she rehashing this, again?

A gust of wind blew tiny icicles that stung her face like knives. She pulled her scarf over the bottom of her face and went on. The forest wasn't much farther, just over the rise covering the steep slope.

She stopped at the edge of the woods and looked at the field she had come through. Her footprints were already covered, only small dimples were left in the snow.

*"Happiness depends upon ourselves."* Mrs. Bainbridge quoted Aristotle to her more than once.

She was right. Disappointment, even betrayal, did not have to color her life. She had been independent and thinking before and she would be that way again.

Mrs. Bainbridge would be shocked. She let out a deep sigh. No, she wouldn't. Mrs. Bainbridge would have her at the seminary dart board taking aim at her problem literally and figuratively.

*"It's good, healthy to have dreams, but you must not confuse them with reality. Dreams are your hopes. You mustn't lose sight of the here and now."*

Mrs. Bainbridge had guided her. She may still have some dreams, but here and now? Here and now she never wanted another man in her life again, ever.

Patrice went on a little further. As she took a step, she knew she was in trouble. Her body moved in one direction, while her foot went in another. Her arms flailed as she struggled to keep her balance, but there was no way she could remain upright. Her walking stick flew from her hands as she tumbled and slid down the steep slope into the pine forest.

The wind blew the snow into drifts that changed the landscape. She must have misstepped. She thought she was clear of the shallow stream that ran down the slope and into the lake.

Her body gathered speed as she slid through the forest. She gasped, realizing a shiver of panic. If she didn't stop soon she'd slide across the small lake and over the cliff. Her hands clawed at the snow, trying to find anything that could slow her down. But all she found was slick ice. *Think. You've slid down slopes at the seminary. You know what to do. Move.* With her momentum building, she rounded the bend and at the top of the curve, she put all her effort into rolling over. She was thrown to the side and off the ice.

Gasping for breath, her heart racing, she lay on her back staring at the gray sky, the snow coming down. At last, she sat up and looked back at the slide marks she left. They were already filling with snow. In the spring the stream flowed north, then turned east to the cliff and into the lake which fed the waterfall, but it was not on this path.

When her heart stopped racing, she got to her feet, brushed off her clothes, and pulled herself along, grasping on branches as she climbed up the incline until she was on level ground. She was on the cliff path to the lodge.

She made her way deeper into the forest where the pine canopy captured the snow and shielded the forest floor. Here the snow wasn't as deep. As she followed the forest path, a pattern of prints in the snow caught her attention, not an animal's, but a human's, prints. Her gaze followed the track. It led toward the lodge.

She hurried on and stopped to bend down for a closer look. Her stomach squeezed. Blood stains spattered the prints. She looked up toward the lodge.

Henry? The wild boar? She stood and checked the sky in the direction of the lodge. No smoke. Was the boy too badly hurt to start a fire?

She took off at a run. Her only thought was Henry.

Her muffled footfalls pounded and crunched on the forest ground as she ran. Afraid of what she'd find when she reached the lodge, she hurried. She pushed dangling branches out of her way as she broke past them, sending a cascade of snow in her wake.

There was only one set of footprints, but the blood stains were getting bigger as she raced along.

Had the boy made it to the lodge? Would she find him buried in the snow?

The gusts of wind picked up as she came to the clearing. The snow was coming down heavily now, making it nearly impossible to see more than a few feet in front of her. She could deal with that, but it covered the prints and blood. If Henry moved off the path, she might not find him in time.

Exhausted, her legs and back aching, she stopped and clung onto a tree as she caught her breath. She didn't usually go to the lodge from this direction but was close.

Moving on, she kept watch through the snow drenched branches and finally made out the faint outline of the lodge ahead. Relieved, she hurried to the building. She wiped the ice from her eyelashes and climbed the steps onto the porch.

Blood stained the lodge door. Without stopping, she hurried inside, ready to help the boy, but she stopped with legs-shaking, heart-straining, chest-tightening, fear.

An unconscious person lay face-down on her sofa.

It wasn't Henry.

# CHAPTER SIX

PATRICE DIDN'T GIVE a thought to who the man might be. Rather, from the amount of blood she saw, she knew he was badly injured and needed help.

With care, she circled around for a better view. His face was buried into the back of the sofa.

He made a low growling sound.

She stepped back and he moved. Perhaps this wasn't a good idea after all, but she couldn't walk out. She forced herself to get closer. He must have been injured by the boar. She took another step as he turned his head and faced her.

Her eyes widened as she stared unblinking into the face of the man who had been with Tanya. The man whose smile sent her heart pounding.

Again, she felt a shadow of recognition, but couldn't put a name to his face.

He mustn't have been here long. His beard was still rimed with ice. She felt his forehead. His skin was cold to the touch, but not frozen.

He winced in pain and slid onto his back. That's when she saw the blood. She pulled off her hat, gloves, and jacket. If she didn't get a fire started soon, they both would freeze. First, she grabbed a fur robe and a few clothes from the cupboard and carefully put the robe over her guest. Satisfied he'd keep some heat, she stacked the wood, placed the tinder, and got the fire started.

"Idi ko mne."

She jumped at his outburst. *Come to me.* She stared at him. In his restlessness, he tossed off the fur. The man looked exhausted with beads of sweat across his forehead. She took one of the cloths and wiped his brow to make him more comfortable.

His eyes fluttered open. They weren't the eyes of a delirious man. They held her in place.

"Mne." His eyelids slid closed.

She stood and looked at him. *To me.*

The room was still cold. She covered him again with the fur. Another glance. Relieved he was alive she went into the kitchen for the kettle.

There was no sense in attempting to use the water pump. She had nothing with which to prime it. Instead, she went outside and filled the kettle with snow. Back in the main room, she slipped the kettle onto the hook that dangled from the lug-pole in the hearth.

While the water heated, she went through the things she brought from the main house, linen, a pot of honey, and small tins of tea and scones. Examining her cache, she realized she never anticipated she would be dressing a major wound. No matter. It would have to do.

Cleaning the wound was essential. From what she saw, more than hot water was needed. She picked up the honey pot.

She had no idea how the man would react to her ministering to him. All she knew – she couldn't leave him as he was.

Patrice knelt next to him and studied his face. His dark, full beard was streaked with silver and glistened from the melted ice. His features, from what she could make out between his beard, cuts, and bruises, were pleasant. He didn't have a tortured grimace but looked rather at peace.

He pushed the fur away. The coat and shirt gaped open and gave her a better look at his wound.

"The bleeding has almost stopped," she said softly, as if he could hear her. "It needs to be cleansed and dressed." He didn't move. "I'll be just a moment."

She hurried out of the room already thinking what needed to be gathered. Her steps slowed as she reached the kitchen. His name taunted her from the edges of her mind, teased her, frustrated her.

*Leave. Now.* The small voice kept at her. *What are you doing? Go now.* What *was* she doing, speaking to the man as if he heard her? Anyone seeing her would think she was…mad. Her mother would—

Cold water on her face couldn't have awakened her more. Her mother would have had him removed without a fare-the-well. Put out on the street, or in this case out into the snow.

That would have been madness.

She rolled her eyes. What was done, was done. A quick turn in the kitchen, then the scullery, and she had what she needed.

Tanya's gentleman was still unconscious when she returned. She let out a breath. *Well, Lady Edgemont, you wanted your independence, your adventure. Now what?*

His quick intake of breath and groan sent her into action.

All she had to do was cleanse his wound and bandage it then she could send him on his way. Steam rose from the water as she poured it from the kettle into the bowl.

She took the clean rags and tore them into strips, put several of them into the hot water, and set the honey next to it. How many times had she watched Mr. Carter attend to her brother? The last time it was a bullet wound in his head, the result of an argument over cards. Even Mr. Carter couldn't fix that. She pushed her brother out of her mind. After a deep breath, she plucked the linen from the bowl and gingerly squeezed out the water, then unfurled the cloth to let it cool a bit.

Now she was ready to take care of her guest. He was quiet, breathing evenly and thankfully, on his back. She touched his forehead. No fever. Careful not to disturb him, she opened his coat and shirt a little further. She picked up the cloth, but before she could apply it, a strong hand grabbed her wrist.

Startled, she stared at the hand grasping hers, then at the man's dazed face.

She had to bend close to hear what he said. It was a jumble of Russian.

"I'm here to help you. You wandered into my lodge."

He tightened his grip. Although she was concerned she wouldn't be able to hold the cloth much longer, she was more concerned about his building anger.

*Think! Something. Anything to quell the fight in his eyes.*

"*Moy lev.* I'm here to help you." *My lion.* It was the only Russian term of endearment that came to mind.

He closed his eyes and released her arm but remained awake.

"Your wound doesn't look deep, but you have lost a lot of blood. I'm going to cleanse and dress it. Are you hungry?"

He gave a nod.

Relieved he understood her, she let out a breath she didn't realize she was holding.

"I noticed you at the tearoom, speaking with Tanya." With care, she placed the warm cloth on his wound and applied a little pressure.

He flinched but said nothing.

"Sorry." She didn't stop. "I'll be as quick as I can. It usually doesn't snow like this here. A few flakes, maybe a dusting on the ground. I can't remember the last time we had a snowstorm." She rinsed the cloth and reapplied it.

He remained quiet. This was going to be a one-way conversation, but that didn't stop her. The conversation was more for her than for him.

"I remember the snow in St. Petersburg. It was a lovely evening." She soaked a clean cloth and applied it.

This time when she removed the cloth she examined the wound more closely. It was a clean cut. The edges of the wound hadn't discolored. He remained still. She didn't think it was made by a wild boar. No. Definitely not made by a wild boar.

"I think that's all for the soaking. Your wound is clean and not deep. Thankfully, I don't think it needs to be stitched up." She glanced at him. His eyes were barely open. "You wouldn't want me to do that anyway. I'm not particularly good with a needle and thread."

The corners of his lips went up a bit and her heart raced.

"What are you good at?" His voice was low, mellow, and familiar.

"You *are* awake. And here I thought I was talking to myself all this time. You are most fortunate. I am very good at slathering honey on my morning toast." She held up the honey pot.

"You paint a very interesting picture, slathering honey."

Patrice felt the heat of her cheeks. His words teased, but it was his sensuous smile that had her lightheaded.

"A rake of the first order. I will have you know that your charms are wasted here, sir." She used her best scolding voice but couldn't stop from smiling.

"You are not concerned, here alone with someone you don't know?"

"You're a friend of Tanya's." She shrugged her shoulders, her lips pursed. "Knowing her, you should be more afraid of what she will do to you if you overstep the boundary."

"You are correct. Tatiana is not someone I want to cross." Again, that smile. "I saw you in the tearoom. With your friends."

She needed to control the conversation.

"The honey."

He gave her a questioning stare.

"You asked about the slathering. The honey is the only thing at hand for your wound. It will keep it clean until you can see a doctor."

She drizzled the honey onto his wound and covered it with a piece of clean dry linen. He sat up and let her wrap a strip of linen around him to keep the dressing in place.

"I'll make us some tea. Would you like to sit here, or do you prefer sitting at the table?" She watched him carefully, not wanting his wound to open.

"I'll sit at the table." The color drained from his face as he stood up. A bit wobbly, he put his arm around her, and they made their way the few yards to the table.

Patrice poured tea and set out the scones along with the jar of honey.

He looked at her quizzically.

"It's either honey or nothing. The cupboard in the lodge is bare." She took a seat across from him and tried to watch him without being intrusive. She was relieved his color returned quickly.

They drank their tea and ate their scones and honey in silence.

"Did you see anyone in the forest?" He'd been in the forest for some time, and perhaps he caught a glimpse of Henry.

He put the cup down. With his elbows on the table, he tented his arms and clasped his hands.

"Why do you ask?" His glare was steady. The playfulness in his voice gone.

"I came to the lodge looking for a lost boy and found an unconscious man sprawled on my sofa with a knife wound." She put her cup down and returned his serious stare. "The only reason I'm still here is because of your association with Tanya."

He said nothing.

"The boy is Henry Percy, Lord Lieutenant Hugh Percy's son. He's gone missing and I'd like to know if you have seen him."

"You put a lot of trust in Tanya. You have no idea who I am."

"And I would like to keep it that way. People with stab wounds are not my usual callers and I think the least I know the better." She got up and began to clear the table but turned as she reached the doorway.

"You're not even curious?" He got up and followed her to the kitchen door.

"Not at all." She lied. She was sure she knew him, but from

where?

"I *am* curious if you've seen anyone in the forest." She held his stare.

"No. I have not."

She went to pass him, but he didn't move. They stood facing each other.

"May I call you Lady Edgemont?"

Her gaze never wavered. "How do you know I'm Lady Edgemont?"

He bent close to her and whispered in her ear. "I asked Tatiana."

Her eyelids slid closed as his warm breath bathed her ear and neck. She became instantly aware of who he was.

He didn't have to ask Tatiana. He knew her as well as she knew him. St. Petersburg. Two years ago.

What was Prince Nikolai Baranov doing dressed as a vagabond and in Sommer-by-the-Sea pretending to be someone else?

# CHAPTER SEVEN

NIKOLAI RETURNED TO the main room. He was playing a deadly game. He found it almost laughable that she didn't recognize him, although there were times he thought…

He stared out the window but caught her reflection as she stood where he left her. He stared past her image at the dense snow. In the distance, he saw the roof of the main house.

It would be nice to remain here, by a warm fire, with Patrice. She was as comfortable to speak with as he remembered. That was a different time. A different place.

No one was safe with him. They killed Philby and would just as easily kill the boy Henry, Lord Percy, even her. No, Patrice and the boy would only be in jeopardy if they found them with *him*. He let out a long breath.

But they had less of a chance of surviving without him.

While Patrice gathered her things in the other room, he surveyed his surroundings. It didn't take much to see that the lodge had been closed for some time. Everything of value was removed, including the weapons. There was no way to defend this location without resources.

"I don't think we can stay here," she said as she returned. "There is no food except for what I brought. Henry wouldn't come here. He'd come to the main house."

It was his turn to stare at her, as she echoed his feelings.

Was she trying to convince him or herself?

"It would be better for you, too," she said.

That piqued his interest.

"Don't look at me like I'm a child. You have a knife wound." She pointed at his chest. "And it wasn't done by accident. Someone is after you. You have little chance of escape here. You'd be better off at the house. Are you strong enough for a walk in the snow?"

That made him chuckle.

"Yes, I would be pleased to walk you to your house. We can look for the boy as well."

"You put out the fire." She gestured to the hearth. "I have a few things to do before we leave."

While she brought everything into the kitchen, he spread out the wood. It hissed and steamed when he poured the last of the water from the kettle onto the embers.

He put on Philby's coat and rifled in the pocket looking for a pair of gloves, instead, he pulled out a note. His eyes widened as he read it quickly.

He looked at the doorway where she had gone. Now he understood why the dying man demanded he take the coat. He tucked the note away. It wasn't the time to think about his mission. It would all come to nothing unless he got them both to safety.

"Are you ready?" Patrice asked as she came back into the room and put on her coat. "The walk to the house is up a steep incline."

"I'll be fine. You lead the way." He was used to great snow-storms and long muffled winters of white nothingness, but this wasn't a pleasure trip. "I'll follow in your footsteps. No need for anyone to know there are two of us."

Lady Edgemont didn't flinch. She nodded her agreement and waited for him at the door.

They left the lodge. The snow, now half-ice pellets, bounced off his coat and was coming down fast. They braced themselves as they moved away from the protection of the building and were caught in the wind, now a horizontal blur.

Sitting inside and watching the storm from the warmth of a hearth one would think the snow was magical. But here, in the thick of it, the snow could be most miserable and deadly.

They trudged along, snow thick on the tree limbs, weighing down the branches. Drifts encased the bushes and rock outcropping, changing the landscape.

Patrice stopped and turned to him.

Her cheeks were flushed. The weak sun reflected on the wisps of her iced tendrils that escaped her red cap. It was as if tiny gems glistened in her hair.

"We're going the long way to avoid an ice hazard. Besides, if Henry was in the area, he would be traveling on it."

He nodded, gestured for her to go on, and followed in her footsteps.

He wasn't surprised at her determination to check for the boy. He wouldn't have expected anything less from her. Edgemont would have taken the same action.

As she veered off the path and moved a few yards ahead of him he followed and felt a different crunch beneath his feet.

"Run. To the woods," he commanded.

She took off without hesitating and turned toward him when she reached the trees.

He was laying on the ground stretched out where he had stood.

She started to come to him.

"No. Stay back. This is all ice and not very thick."

She pulled her foot back. In the quiet, she heard the ice cracking. God's toes, she chose this path because there was no water. She put her hand on the surface. The ice vibrated.

They both watched as the ice shifted. It was breaking apart.

"THAT CAN'T BE. There is no water here. The stream is..." She looked toward the top of the rise. This explained why she tumbled down the slope before. Some of the stream was diverted. It's what the magistrate mentioned earlier.

She couldn't let him lay there much longer. Each cracking sound had her concerned he would fall through. Getting him out of the icy water would be near impossible for her. She pulled off her scarf, examining it for its length.

"This will have to do," she mumbled.

Patrice found a sizeable rock and wrapped it onto one end of her scarf.

She hefted the wool-covered rock, satisfied with her work. She went to the edge of the ice.

"Grab the scarf when I toss it to you. I'll pull you off."

"I don't think that will be as easy as you think," he said.

She ignored his comment and tossed it towards him. It was short. She pulled it back and threw it again. Better, but still short. The third time she put more effort into it. It looked like it would fly over him except he reached up and caught it.

"Hold tight," she said and wrapped the end around her arm and tried to pull. He didn't budge. She tried again and heard the wool stretch and tighten but discounted it. The ice would give way before she got back to the house, found a rope, and got back here. No. That wasn't an option. This was all she had.

She stepped back, put her foot on the nearest boulder, and pulled on the scarf, hand-over-hand.

He used his free hand and pulled on the ice and inched toward her. The small push forward he created was what she needed. She kept at it, reeling him like a fish she wanted to bring to shore.

He crawled off the ice. Exhausted. She collapsed next to him.

"Are you all right?" He was out of breath.

"I should be asking you that." She glanced at him. "My arms feel like they are twice as long as they should be. Other than that, I'm fine."

They rested only a few minutes, then went on.

As they came around a bend, he grabbed her arm and pulled her back.

"What is it?" She glanced ahead searching for what caught his attention.

He didn't say anything, simply nodded to their right.

The snow covered a recent disturbance, but it was a piece of snagged cloth on the branch that held his attention. He pulled it off.

"I don't have to look closely. The men I'm after aren't careless. This is their way of leaving me a message."

"Message?"

He handed her the tattered cloth. It had a familiar emblem.

Her face grew pale. Her breathing rapid.

"This is from a livery uniform." She turned it over and drew in a deep breath. "It's the Montgomery crest." Her gaze went from the scrap to his eyes.

He saw so many questions in them.

"What does this mean?" Her voice dropped to a whisper.

"They are near. Neither of us is safe."

# CHAPTER EIGHT

Tired, out of breath, and cold, he and Patrice made their way up the rise to the gate at the back of the garden. The walk, even with the diversion on the ice, should never have taken so much out of him. But he pushed on, refusing to give into exhaustion. He concentrated on walking in Patrice's steps, thinking about how he underestimated the opposition and walked into the trap in Philby's office like a lamb to slaughter.

"Henry must be at the house." She pointed to the open gate up ahead.

"There's no telling when this was done." He knew she had been in London for months and no one had been here.

"I came through the garden when I left the house for the lodge." She turned toward him. "I locked it when I left."

A flicker of apprehension rushed through him. The scrap of cloth bothered him.

"I didn't hear or see anything out of place. There were no footprints at the main entrance when I arrived. The only prints I saw out here when I left were animal tracks." They moved closer to the gate.

He pulled her behind him before she bolted forward.

On alert, he scanned the area for anything that was out of place.

"What about the scrap of cloth? How do we explain that?"

"Father had the crest remade when my brother, Brian, died. This is the old one. Father's solicitor removed all the livery and gave them away. It could be anyone's."

"Were you told someone was with the boy?" He nodded toward the ground.

Patrice followed his gaze and stared at the two different sets of footprints on the path. One set deeper than the other.

"You're sure you closed the gate?" He couldn't see much of the garden and from where they were the high garden wall hid the house.

"Yes." Her unsettled voice whispered behind him. "You don't think someone would—"

"Enter your home uninvited? Unannounced?" His gaze never left the gate. "Yes, I am certain of it."

He muttered a stream of Russian curses under his breath. His next move had to be planned carefully. Patrice couldn't stay alone in the house, or at the lodge, and he certainly wasn't going to leave her out here while he investigated the garden. He needed her full cooperation. How was a vagabond going to accomplish that?

"What if it is Henry, or someone who is in trouble?" she asked.

"You must hope for the best but prepare for the worst," was his off-handed remark. He was concentrating on how to keep her safe.

She gave him an odd stare. "You're familiar with Thomas Norton's writing?"

The shock of possible discovery hit him full-force. He should have known she would recognize the quotation from the 16th century play, *The Tragedie of Gorbuduc*. It wasn't the most well-known phrase, but it had struck a chord with him, and obviously with her as well.

"But I understand your meaning." She didn't wait for his response.

"I'll take you to the Manning estate. You'll be safe there." Yes.

That would be the best solution.

Her head whipped around. Her eyes glowed with a savage inner fire.

"I overheard that the Manning estate was near The Mooring when I was at the tearoom." Another mistake like that could cost him dearly.

Her temper cooled. "I will not stand by idly and let intruders roam through my house like someone at the village market. Do I make myself clear?"

He admired her pride and commitment but remained concerned about her safety.

"Let's hope there will be no need to remove people from your house or move you to the Manning estate. We'll enter the garden. No matter what I say, you must do as I ask. Both our lives, even Henry's if they have him, may depend on it. Do you understand?"

Patrice nodded.

If he expected to see fear in her eyes, he was disappointed.

"Tell me what I must do." Determination touched with a bit of anger glowed on her face.

The tension in his shoulders eased. For a moment he feared she would argue with him taking command. He was relieved when she didn't. That was one hurdle behind him. He wished he knew how many more he faced.

They moved toward the garden wall to examine the gate and area around it.

"Someone chopped away at the wood and the lock." He ran his hand over the damaged area of the gate.

"This was all perfectly fine and working when I left." She stood staring at the damage. Finally, she turned to him. "I'm surprised we didn't hear someone chopping away at it."

"This snow muffles the sound. It must have been done while you were in the lodge." He glanced at the ground.

Small swirls of snow had been blown in all directions. Thankfully, the wind had cleared a good part away from the wall. He brushed the ground with his foot, concentrating on the small mounds until he found what he was looking for.

"What's that?" Patrice peered over his shoulder.

"An improvised key to your gate." He picked up a small axe and handed it to her.

"Whoever they were, they took it from the lodge." Patrice stared at him her mouth agape as she showed him the handle. "The Edgemont Crest. This axe is kept near the lodge woodpile in the back. I brought you here on the steep path from the lodge. The path these men took, the one that joined ours is from the back of the lodge."

There had been no activity around the lodge when he got there, or so he thought. In his state he may not have been as thorough as he liked. The idea made him uncomfortable. He cursed himself for not thinking to search the area before they left.

These men were ahead of him, not behind. They must have arrived at the lodge before him. He could have overlooked their footprints. The snow was coming down thick and the wind whipped it around.

That didn't matter now. He had to deal with what they faced.

"Tell me about the garden," he said, staring through the gate.

"There are three areas. Entering here, we'll be at the top of the maze. To the right is the kitchen herb garden. To the left is the ornamental and rose gardens. The only entrances to the garden are through the gate and the house."

He stared past the gate into the garden. Two, maybe three, yards beyond the gate he could make out a wall of yew hedges, the branches thick with snow, but that wasn't what caught his attention. The footprints went through the yews. The intruders had entered the maze.

"Stay close. We'll follow their trail into the maze and see where they lead."

"Here, you take this." She handed him the axe and picked up a piece of wood broken off from the gate. "I wouldn't know what to do with that."

He hefted the axe. It wasn't a bad weapon, but he hoped he wouldn't have to use it. Then they both squeezed through the gap in the gate.

Before they went any further, she pulled the gate closed as best she could.

"Why bother?"

"I was told there was a wild boar in the area. The last thing we need is the intruders in front of us and a wild animal behind."

He nodded. She remained close behind him as they got deeper into the maze.

"These tracks are recent." Patrice knelt for a closer look. "The snow hasn't completely covered them."

He had to agree with her. She was more observant than he expected.

"There is no hesitation at the intersections." Her gaze followed the tracks until they disappeared around a turn. "The tracks go on as if these people know where they are going. See how they go right through the intersections."

He stopped when they came to the intersection and strained to listen. Here, as well as in the forest, the snow and high hedge walls muffled the sounds. Nothing and he wasn't sure if that was a good sign or a bad one. All he could do is move them on toward their objective until they came to another decision point.

Whether he was on the offense or defense in battle didn't matter. It was who controlled the moves. He wasn't in control here and needed to turn that around, or make it into his advantage.

Patrice tapped his shoulder.

He stopped but kept his eyes trained ahead.

"They're not looking for a way out of the maze."

"Why do you say that?" He glanced at her over his shoulder.

"The people we're tracking appear to know the maze. If I'm correct, they know the way out. It's to the left. This direction," she nodded pointing where the footprints led, "goes to the center."

"Unless they made a mistake or finished what they are doing and have to double back in this direction." He felt her soft breath on the back of his neck. "Keep close and stay alert."

He slowed their pace, concentrated, and listened. This situation was not optimum. His only weapon was the axe, he had Patrice to protect, and the space was small. His only advantage would be the element of surprise.

Patrice pulled on his arm. He turned and followed her gaze. The hedge had been disturbed. Broken branches under a thin layer of snow suggested—

"Someone came through the hedge wall." He was impressed with her observations and glad she was with him but still worried about her safety.

With care, he poked his head through the hedge then pulled it back.

"There's another set of footprints on the other side. Whomever was there joined the two on this side."

She looked through the hedge. "How would you know that?"

"Look at the footprints in front of us. Two sets a bit apart and something dragged between them."

They continued on the twisting path without any further revelations.

"The next intersection is the central avenue of the maze. To the right we should be able to see into the heart of the maze. It's one of my favorite places on the estate." She nodded to the right.

"And to the left?" He stared to the left.

"To the left there are twists and turns but no other intersecting paths. It leads to the way out."

"Whomever we are following didn't leave by the exit." Why go to the center of the maze? Was it a meeting place? He glanced at the top floor of the building. It may have been better if they'd gone directly into the house and done their investigation from up there.

Patrice moved around him and searched the ground. She straightened and faced him.

"There are no footprints on that part of the path. We had best go see who is in the center, but not that way. Come with me."

"Where are we going?" He held her back.

"The adjacent path. The hedge is thinner here. We should be able to make our way through the hedge without much difficulty."

He followed her. The hedge thinned and he saw the pavilion on the other side. His pace slowed. The scene on the other side of the hedge appeared to be serene. Too serene. From where he stood he could see tracks in the snow leading into the pavilion.

"I'll go first," he said as he hefted the axe. With care he made his way to the small clearing. Empty. Before he could stop her, Patrice came through the hedge and was next to him.

They stood in the center and took stock of the area. The ground was riddled with footprints. Blood splattered and stained the snow. It was concentrated in a trail leading into the pavilion.

"Stay here." He started for the small building.

"Oh, no. I'm right behind you." She followed so close she nearly stepped on the heel of his boots.

His eyes were everywhere, alert for an attack.

Inside the pavilion everything looked as it should, except for a man's body draped across the stone bench at the back wall. His right arm hung down. The back of his hand was in the snow that was tinged red.

He hurried to the man. He had no illusions. He'd seen enough lifeless bodies to know the man was dead. Other than the errant arm hanging over the edge, the other arm was bent across his chest. The legs were straight. Even the coat was pulled closed. The body had been placed on the bench for them to find.

He touched the tips of his fingers to the side of the man's neck although it wasn't necessary. He stepped back.

Patrice came up beside him. He looked for something to cover the man, but he had nothing. There was no way he could protect her from seeing this horror.

She gasped.

He swung around. "Are you all right?"
Patrice nodded her head. Her eyes held a startled sheen.
"I know him," she mumbled.

# CHAPTER NINE

NIKOLAI PUT HIS arm around Patrice. She was shaking all over. He glanced at the man trying to understand how Patrice and the dead man were connected.

"That's Joseph Peters. Edgemont's former solicitor. He was not an… honest man." Her voice was fragile and void of emotion. "If you don't mind, I'll wait for you by the steps."

She slipped away to the pavilion steps where she stared out into the garden. There was no shame in her removing herself from the gruesome scene.

He looked at the corpse. Osip Petrova. He didn't know the man well only that he had left St. Petersburg and was a solicitor in London.

So this was Peters. He had heard about the man's disgrace. But why was a dead solicitor in his former employer's garden maze?

When he first saw Peters, he was concerned about Patrice's reaction. He glanced over his shoulder. She was doing fine. Now he looked at the area more closely. There was little disturbance in the snow around the bench. Some blood, but not much. More reason to believe the man was already dead when he was put here.

He examined Peters' clothes and found a tear. He took out the tattered cloth from the branch. It fit in the torn area.

A smear of blood on the coat did not surprise him. The murderer cleaned off his blade after the fatal blow. He recognized that calling card. He glanced at the pavilion exit and was relieved that Patrice remained there. He continued to examine the body.

The sleeves of the man's coat were slashed, blood on the edges of the cut material. In his mind's eye he could see Peters with his arms raised protecting himself as the attack rained down on him.

He carefully examined the hand that hung down. The palm and fingers were severely lacerated. At one point, Peters must have grasped the blade. The wrists were not compromised. These wounds were not fatal.

He stepped around the bench and stopped. Peters did not die easily. He pushed the blood-soaked cravat away and found a short slash, across his neck, long and shallow. He stood up. This too, was not a killing wound.

Peters' coat, while not buttoned, was wrapped around him. It was as if the arm across his chest held it closed. He moved the arm and the coat gapped open. He pushed the edge of the lapel to the side and exposed the man's torso. His shirt was in shreds and bloody.

He came to his full height. His eyes stared at Peters but saw another time. He was only a boy when he had been forced to watch a similar execution. His cousin convinced him it was a part of war.

He was groomed to take over the family business. But his father's growing political position required he remain removed from the operation. Distant cousins stepped in. But both were adamant that Nikolai learn every aspect.

He excelled at handling the accounts, keeping track of goods, money, and anything else that needed documenting. The position suited him, and he would have been quite content remaining where he was. But his father wanted him to learn it all, so he went off with his cousins.

He naively thought they were meeting a business partner.

The man was demanding, but Nikolai thought there was room to negotiate. His cousins would have none of that. He made his demands. Words were spoken, tempers flared, and his cousin's knife flashed.

Too shocked to move or speak, he watched in horror. The torture, execution, and the knife wiped on the man's coat stained his mind as badly as the black ink from the account books stained his fingers.

Over time, the image faded until two years ago when he saw the results of another execution. The results of that killing would be with him forever.

He gave himself a shake and came back to the present. He needed to get his investigation over and move Patrice to safety.

A quick search of the man's pockets resulted in several coins and a wad-up piece of linen. The weight of the cloth told him something was tucked inside.

There was no telling if or when the killers might return. He didn't want to be here armed only with an axe especially with Patrice. He slipped the item into his coat, returned the coins to Peters' pocket, and walked over to Patrice.

"I may know who did this. But at the moment, Mr. Joseph Peters will have to wait. We're too vulnerable here. As far as we know two men remain at large. I want to get you inside."

She nodded. They left the pavilion and walked the avenue path. They came out of the maze and went to the right, toward the kitchen herb garden. He held out his hand when they reached the door. She gave him the key.

"We can sit in the parlor." The key turned easily, and he opened the door.

"Not at the moment. I want to check the house and make sure it is secure." They stepped in and he closed and locked the door behind him.

"Secure? Of course the house is secure." Patrice stood in front of him dumbfounded. "The garden is one thing, but no one would dare..."

"There are those who would dare. I have this overwhelming desire to live to a ripe old age and will do all that I can to make that happen. Therefore, I will check the house."

Her red hair paled in comparison to the fire that ignited when she was determined.

"Not without me. I will defend what is mine." Her chest heaved. "The idea that someone forced their way into my home is maddening."

"If you insist, we will do it together."

She inclined her head in agreement. She lit the candelabra by the door, and took him through the servant's hall, to the grand staircase.

"We want to start at the top floor, in a room that has a view of the maze."

"The nursery would be the best room. Why do you want to look down at the maze?"

"Rather than spend a great deal of time in the cold, I'd like to see the entire picture of where those other footprints lead."

"Me as well." She led him up the stairs. "The house has been closed for the last ten months. All the shutters were closed, and the hearth dampers shut throughout the house."

"Then it shouldn't take us long to go through each room and make sure they remained secure." They reached the top floor. She took him to the middle of a long hall.

"This room has the most complete view of the garden." She reached for the latch, but he grabbed it first and pushed her to the side. She swung around ready to reprimand him.

"Patrice. Don't fight me on this. I will enter the rooms first and make sure they are safe. Leave the candle in the hall. I don't want anyone outside seeing lights moving about on the upper floors."

He specifically used her given name and spoke with authority to make her stop. She steamed at his bravado but did as he asked and that was all that mattered at the moment.

He went to the window but didn't open the shutters. Instead, he looked through the louvers at the maze below. She stood at his side.

"The footprints lead to the rose garden. I don't see any indication that they return," she said. "There is no way to get out if you go through the rose garden."

He moved closer to the shutter. "The snow on the top of the wall, by the overhanging branch, is disturbed. They must have gotten out by going over the wall."

He stepped away. There was time enough to track them after he was sure she was safe. He didn't think they were after her. It was him they wanted.

"I want to check the other rooms."

She took him to each room. He examined them from the closed shutters to the closets. The lack of housekeeping over the months was in their favor. The dust and cobwebs in the rooms had not been disturbed. Everything seemed to be in order.

They finished their examination below stairs.

The tension that had driven her drained away and left her exhausted. Their search confirmed that there were no intruders. Nothing was out of place.

Patrice took him into the parlor and led him to the wing-back chair next to the hearth. She stirred the fire back to life and turned to him.

"Rest and let me look at that wound." The woman was determined. Nothing he did would stop her.

"I'm not tired." His heavy eyelids that involuntarily drifted shut told another story. "The wound is fine."

"Have you looked at your shirt? I'm not sure if you're bleeding or if it just stained from before." She took a small pillow from the sofa and tucked it behind his head. "I won't be long."

While Patrice was gone he removed the wad of linen he took from Peters' pocket and placed it on the small side table and began to untie the knots that held it together and peeled it open.

Rumors about Peters' dismissal from Edgemont's employ circulated in legal circles in England and the continent. He became a person with whom no upstanding gentleman would do business. If he was no longer employed by the business, what was he doing at Edgemont's estate? In the old Montgomery livery?

The more he worked the knots on the cloth the more he imagined he'd find a key. Probably a worthless one that led to the man's flat. He was about to give up when he loosened the last knot.

When he got to the prize he sat back in astonishment.

This was not a good omen. His eyes flashed at the door where she had vanished. Had Patrice expected Peters? Was her portrait of vulnerability, alone without any staff, a sham? Was this another trap?

He could never believe Patrice had been involved in her husband's business in Russia. He was betting his life on it.

He had no illusions. If he had to, he would do what was necessary to complete his assignment and hoped Patrice was not involved or worse, an obstacle that he had to remove.

A movement in the hall made him put the linen and its contents back into his pocket. He sat back in the chair and waited. He didn't have to wait long.

# CHAPTER TEN

Patrice returned with a tray of medical supplies and found him at ease in Edgemont's chair. She worked hard at giving off the same relaxed appearance.

Her friends would think her daring while her mother would believe she'd lost all her senses. Alone with a man. To say nothing of a dead body in the garden pavilion.

Patrice gazed at him poised in the large leather chair as if he belonged there as she crossed the room. She didn't know why he played at being someone else but decided to wait until he disclosed his identity.

His easy banter appealed to her. His playful sense of humor appealed to her. His good looks touched with a hint of danger appealed to her. God's toes, she must be mad.

She set the tray on the table.

He undid the shirt buttons and leaned forward. She helped him peel it off. One look and she stood back without a sound.

"I should have warned you. A casualty of the French invading Moscow."

She didn't give him pity nor did she look on in horror.

"Most would not have endured such brutality. You did." She wanted to tell him how brave he'd been but held her tongue concerned he would find it a trivial remark.

"It's not a pretty sight."

No. It wasn't. How had she not noticed beyond the muscular well-defined torso silvery scars that crisscrossed his chest? He had been beaten, badly beaten. No wonder he was so stoic about his current condition. She could only imagine how he suffered. She seethed at the injustice, no one deserved to be treated in this manner. Determined not to embarrass him more, she set her mind to taking care of him and looked past the rest.

She untied the bandage and removed the dressing, ready for the worst. A sigh of relief escaped her lips.

"There's no bleeding," she muttered.

"Of course there isn't. You're an excellent nurse."

At first she thought he jested, but when she glanced at him there wasn't any sign of his teasing nature. He was serious.

"Where did you learn your medical skills?" he asked as she examined the wound.

"My friend is a doctor and taught several of us some emergency skills."

"He must be quite good. You're better than the field doctors I'm familiar with."

"She. Dorothea is a she. And yes, Dorothea is excellent at what she does."

"I've never heard of a woman doctor." Patrice smiled at the surprise in his voice. "Her father will admit she is a better doctor than he is."

"That explains your skill. You are an excellent nurse because you learned from the best."

"I will graciously accept your compliment." She tilted her head in acknowledgement. "I'll clean you up a bit more and apply some salve."

"No honey?" There was that smile in his voice that warmed her.

"You'll have to find another use for it."

"I'm sure I can think of something." His voice was low and sensual.

She gave him a quizzical look as she recounted her words.

Her eyes widened and a flush of color rushed to her cheeks.

"Forgive me," he chuckled. "I should have remained quiet. I didn't mean to make you uncomfortable."

She gathered her composure. His playfulness was refreshing. Brian had warned her about her wry sense of humor. How it could be misinterpreted even by the best of men. But her guard was down with him. Nor did she feel vulnerable. Not even with the man half-undressed.

"As I was saying, I have a healing salve that would serve you better. That along with a fresh bandage will have you as good as new in no time."

Ministering to him wasn't as easy as she thought. She cleansed the area. He wasn't the issue, it was her. The closeness to him, the intimacy of her actions, unnerved her.

*Keep your mind on what needs to be done, not some fanciful imagining.*

"You live here, not in London," he said. He gazed at her as she applied the salve.

She stopped and looked at her work, satisfied with what she saw.

"I prefer to stay here rather than at Edgemont Arms." She continued to care for his wound.

Touching him sent shock waves through her. She didn't linger, she wouldn't dare. Finished, at last, she wiped her hands and took up the bandage.

"I don't blame you. It is peaceful."

"It's why I returned here." He held the linen against his wound as she wrapped the bandage around him and tied it off. She stepped back and looked at her handiwork. "Mr. Regis, my butler, would do a much better job, but it should do for now. You must be hungry. Tea and scones aren't enough. I'll make us something to eat." She gathered the supplies and made ready to leave.

"A lady who is a nurse and a cook. Let me help you. It's the least I can do." He got to his feet and offered his arm to her.

His gallant gesture took her by surprise and sent a flash of heat rushing up her neck, warming her cheeks. She looked at his outstretched arm then at his face. This man was more aristocrat than vagabond, down to his well-cared for fingernails.

He took her arm, tucked it over his, and escorted her down the central stairs to the servants' hall as if they were entering the throne room at the palace.

He went directly to the stove, lifted the pot cover as if he was the house chef, and let out a hearty laugh.

"Just as I thought, mushroom barley soup." He turned toward her.

"Mrs. Chernokov sent me home with it. She knows the soup is my favorite. Hers has a special flavor that I thoroughly enjoy."

*Snow was falling as the carriage made its way through the streets of St. Petersburg. Edgemont was called to the palace. He insisted that she and Nikolai enjoy dinner and that he would see her later.*

*"You'll enjoy The Palkin. It is one of the finest dining rooms in the city." Prince Baranov escorted her to the carriage after the ballet.*

*"Yes, the countess told me about its Russian cuisine. I'm looking forward to dinner." She was accustomed to being without Edgemont, but a dinner party or gala, not out. Having the prince's full attention was exhilarating.*

*"I'll order for you if you like and arrange for a variety of Russian food for you to sample."*

*She nodded, relieved he understood her situation.*

*"What does the chef make that you enjoy?" She settled into her seat.*

*"Some would say I have a peasant's taste."*

*"You've piqued my interest." She entertained Edgemont's business associates, but always with him. She had no idea what to expect from this arrangement but hoped the evening would go quickly. Baranov's informal conversation surprisingly put her at ease, too much at ease.*

*"Hearty mushroom barley soup."*

*She spun around on the seat and faced him. "You're not jesting, are you? I'm very fond of mushroom barley soup."*

*"No, not at all. My nyanya made the best mushroom barley soup.*

*She had a bowl ready for my sister and me when we returned from our escapades in the snow. She enjoyed snowball fights." He leaned in closer to her. "There's always snow in St. Petersburg in the winter.*

*"'Eat,' Olga, our nyanya, would say. 'It will make you strong, like bull, moy lev,'" he said with an exaggerated Russian accent.*

*"Moy lev?"*

*"My lion. A term of endearment from my childhood. Did you have a pet name?"*

*"No. My friends call me Patrice." She stared at him.*

*"Patrice is a good strong name. But, let me see. With your red hair, lishichka is more fitting."*

*"Dare I ask what that means?"*

*"Lishichka. Little fox," His voice was soft and mellow.*

*The intimate expression and passion in his eyes startled and excited her. She lowered her eyes and turned away breathless.*

*"Do you still enjoy Olga's soup?" She didn't look at him, afraid he would see more than she was willing to disclose.*

*"My sister Anya and I could never get enough of the snow or Olga's soup."*

That evening was a lifetime ago. She wasn't in St. Petersburg now, but rather in the kitchen of her own country home. She set the table in the servant's dining hall and laid out a dish of salt, cheese, and bread. She started to return to the kitchen but as she passed the cupboard with the crystal glasses, she set out two and looked at the wine cabinet. She passed up the sherry for the brandy. Satisfied with the table, she returned to the kitchen.

"Did you have your tea leaves read?" He ladled the soup into the bowls.

"In a moment of weakness, I let Tanya read them. She told me it would snow. No," she stopped for a moment, a puzzled look on her face that brightened, "she predicted a blizzard."

He poured the last ladle into the bowls and glanced out the window. "The woman was always very perceptive."

"She said I would have good fortune then something about anchors, palm trees, triangles, and hearts."

"All positive signs, I'm sure." He held out her chair and she sat down.

"Ah, you also know how to read the tea leaves."

What in heaven's name was she doing? Her mother would send for smelling salts if she had any idea she was sitting in the servant's dining hall and eating with a vagabond prince. The excitement and adventure made her feel alive. Something she hadn't felt since…St. Peterburg.

Why then? She had so much promise for that journey. After the robbery, they whisked her away quickly, for her own protection. At least that's what Edgemont said.

The count argued he was needed at some meeting in several weeks. He was told since his villa was compromised it would be best for him and the countess to leave the country. They were to escort her back to England. Edgemont was adamant he would see her off. They rode to the harbor in silence. He took her to her stateroom.

He paced the room in deep thought. She wondered if he remembered she was there. He stopped and gave her his attention. He began to talk and crammed much into the short time they had left.

An apology for not being with her the night before.

A promise to explain all.

An oath he would find and return her jewelry.

A kiss that was interrupted.

A smile she hadn't seen in a long time lit his face.

And then he was gone.

It all happened so quickly. As the ship pulled away, she stood at the rail looking down at Edgemont and waved farewell. She had no idea it would be forever.

She glanced across the table. There was no denying that for the first time since Edgemont's murder, she felt alive. Her heart pounded with excitement and anticipation as it did years ago, and she wasn't willing to squash it. She didn't want to examine the reasons for this feeling, nor discourage it. No, she wanted it to last as long as possible. As much as she craved for it to go on, she needed the truth.

At the end of the meal, Patrice poured brandy into a fine crystal glass and handed it to her guest.

He gazed at her.

"Brandy. To warm your insides and ease the pain." She looked up at the ceiling then put the glass to her lips. "Na zdrovie."

"Na zdrovie za druchbu. To a wonderful evening," he responded. His summer-sky blue eyes stared at her over the rim of the glass.

Too startled by his words to say anything. He remembered and more memories of dinner at the Palkin flooded into her mind.

*"This is vodka, a traditional Russian drink. It has a long history. It was produced for medicinal reasons, but it was found to have other benefits."*

*"Such as?"*

*He looked at her with mischief in his eyes.*

*"Is it some Russian secret?"*

*"Not at all. In the early days, vodka was used as a medicine. In the mid-16*th *century, a Polish physician botanist claimed vodka," he leaned close to her, "increased fertility and awakened lust."*

*The breathiness of his gentle, whispered voice sent tingles down her spine. She turned and faced him. He didn't move. He remained close, so close she could feel his breath against her cheeks.*

*He lowered his lids, the trace of a smile on his lips made her heart thunder. Reckless? Yes.*

*She had gone too far and increased the distance between them. The moment passed. The encouragement was her doing. She knew better than to tease, but for a moment...*

*"There are three fundamental things one must do prior to drinking vodka."*

*Baranov continued as if nothing happened. For that, she was grateful. While she composed herself, Baranov spoke about the fundamentals.*

*There was no judgement, only a small sense of regret on his part. Or perhaps that was what she wanted to see.*

"So, Lady Edgemont, I honor the Spirit." *Nikolai took a deep breath, glanced at the ceiling, and teased his lips with the vodka. She did the same.*

*"Na zdrovie za druchbu, to a wonderful evening," he said.*

*"Na zdrovie za druchbu, to a wonderful evening," she repeated then took a sip.*

The image of the Palkin faded. At the moment, she couldn't tell which sparkled more, the crystal glass or his eyes.

"One should never drink alone." He gestured toward the glass in her hand. "I wonder if that mid-16th century Polish physician botanist would claim French brandy also increased fertility and awakened lust."

She looked past the beard, the silvery strands in his hair and into his eyes. Why was he here? What did he want from her? Edgemont's business?

"Nikolai? I thought it was you," she whispered under her breath. *I hoped it was you.*

His face lit in that smile that heated her to the core.

*God's thumb, I'm lost.*

# CHAPTER ELEVEN

PATRICE RAISED HER glass and brought it to her lips. Her eyes that held a burning faraway look moments ago were cold and assessing. She put the glass down without taking a drink.

Her cut was painful. He should have known better than to expect her to accept his small deception. Well, perhaps it wasn't so small. Justifying his actions would get him nowhere, instead, he buried his regret and refused to display any remorse.

"I'm confused." He didn't miss the determination in her voice. "You have the manners and air of a Russian nobleman yet the presence of a vagabond? I prefer to know who I am entertaining or in this case, to whom I'm giving shelter."

He remained silent and took in every nuance of her movement and expressions. Patrice's attitude held without any break, not even a small crack.

"You know who I am." He kept his tone even and controlled not at all sure what she would do.

"I thought I would know you anywhere. It's obvious that you have fooled me as others have." She paused a moment, still looking into his eyes. "I will not be fooled again."

He saw her raw hurt and said nothing. What was there to say? Beg her for forgiveness? No, nothing he said would make the situation better.

"Yes, I know who you are, the son of Grand Duke Anton

Stephanovich Baranov of the House of Breuce."

"The late Grand Duke," he said softly and watched Patrice's eyes widen. It was the only emotion she allowed him to see.

"My sincere condolences. Does that make you the new Grand Duke of Breuce?"

He nodded.

"How does one greet a Russian Grand Duke? Do I bow?"

He said nothing. It would be best for him to let her go on.

"Did you enjoy your little charade?"

He endured her tirade without any comment.

"What made you come to me? What made you think I would be eager to see you?"

In truth, he was on his way to meet his contact and was told the lodge was a safe place to go should he need it. He had no idea the lodge belonged to Edgemont. According to the information he had, Patrice was in London and wouldn't be returning to the village until the summer.

Nikolai endured the rest of her constrained rant that painted him as some sort of lecherous rogue until she ran out of words.

"Are you finished?" He didn't hide his annoyance.

She turned away and dismissed him with a wave of her hand.

He took the linen from his pocket and placed its contents in front of her.

Patrice turned and reached for her brandy but stopped, her hand poised by the glass.

"Where did you get..." A faint hint of hysteria was in her voice as she looked at him.

"You'll have to ask your Mr. Peters. It was in his pocket."

He picked up the diamond and ruby pin and examined it closely.

"I'm not a jeweler, but I know enough about this piece in particular and precious stones in general to know these are genuine." He replaced the brooch in front of her. "I thought this was stolen from Count Pushchin's residence. No one could understand how a thief could get in and out of your room or the residence with the gem and remain unseen. Perhaps it wasn't stolen at all. Did you give it to Peters? Was he returning it to you?"

"I haven't seen the brooch since the Tzar showed it to me at the palace on April twelfth, to be exact. Why would I give it away? And to Peters? I can't think of any reason why Mr. Peters would have it unless he..." She stared at him. "You said you thought you knew who murdered him."

"When your husband came back from the palace he had it and put it in your jewel case. In the morning when he went to get it, the pin was gone. Can you explain that?"

"I was the victim, not the thief. And I will remind you that all my jewelry was taken." She met his icy gaze with defiance.

"I understand your jewelry, without this pin was returned to you." He watched her carefully as she realized how that fact could be damaging.

"No, things aren't always as they appear," was his slow, careful response.

He watched as she mulled that over. Her defenses softened.

Patrice wasn't the enemy, and she had every right to be suspicious of him. He was the one that was stabbed and bleeding when she stumbled upon him in her lodge, but how much dare he confide in her?

"I see your meaning. We are both dealing with misconceptions." She took a sip of the brandy.

"Let me start at the beginning." He sat back, a serious expression on his face.

"Yes, please do, but not here. I prefer to continue our discussion in the parlor."

She didn't wait for him to agree. She picked up the two glasses of brandy and left the room, leaving the gem on the table.

He grabbed the bottle of brandy and followed.

If she knew the significance of the gem, she was a good actor. Edgemont told him she knew nothing about the piece, and he agreed.

They sat in front of the hearth across from each other. He had been in many precarious situations, but never one with consequences that meant so much to him.

He leaned forward. His elbows on his thighs, the glass in his hands.

"Your husband's family and mine have a long history. Both are acknowledged for their military strategy and have on occasion worked together."

"You knew my husband well?"

He took a moment to answer. "Not as well as I would have liked." His voice was quiet and somber. "My position in my father's business was liaison between the families."

Patrice said nothing. He had no idea what she was thinking.

"We both had lucrative business with France."

"Oh, I understand. Your business and his maneuvered around the embargo."

That made him smile. She was a bright woman. "We both kept our trading options open and did the best to give our customers what they needed. Even after Napoleon was banished to Elba Island. Edgemont often visited the emperor as a welcome guest."

"Napoleon? Why?"

"Businessmen, for the most part, don't take political sides. Edgemont was one of those men."

"And you? Did you visit the emperor?"

"No. He was not fond of the English, but absolutely hated the Russians. We were a reminder of his defeat. With the family business arrangement in place, when needed, Edgemont traveled to Elba."

Her startled face settled into a determined expression.

"I've been through his business papers and dealings. There is nothing there to suggest that he was involved with Napoleon or Elba."

"Edgemont was precise in his record keeping. It's all there listed as Suprême or Fleur de Lis Enterprise with a Holland address."

"Yes. I remember those accounts. They sent me a post expressing their sympathy. I thought it was very touching. But now, after what you just said, I wonder if it was to keep their good price."

He chuckled at her nonchalant attitude.

"That's possible, but I'm sure the spirit of the message is simply what they wrote. Edgemont was well liked."

Her chest heaved at the slight reprimand, or was it enlightenment? Edgemont was better than he thought. He kept his business dealings separate from his private life.

Now, in order for him to succeed, he needed her to come to grips with who Edgemont really was. After all the man sacrificed, he owed him that much.

"There were several letters I read on my journey here from people whose names I didn't recognize. I assume they were business associates." She took a breath. "I didn't receive all the letters and cards until recently. There was a card from the Grand Duke of Breuce. I thought it was your father."

"I was in London and wanted to pay my respects."

She was barely able to control a gasp of surprise.

"I thank you for your concern, but after what you've told me, how you know Edgemont and a bit of his dealings with Bonaparte, did you have another reason to speak to me?"

"A situation at my father's business had me doubting who I could trust. I didn't have faith in anyone representing the family in London with our clients or with a client's recent widow."

Her thoughts were on her face. She accepted his words but was aware he hadn't answered her question. For the moment, she let the question pass.

He got up and poured himself more brandy and held out the bottle to her in question.

She handed him her glass.

"You haven't told me why the brooch is important, why you're here, dressed as a vagabond, or why there is a dead body in my garden. When you're finished with your explanation, I will tell you if I trust you or toss you out and let you fend for yourself."

He had to stop himself from laughing. Her matter-of-fact manner sounded as if she found dead bodies in her garden every day. As for being tossed out, he imagined she could manage it. She was entitled to an explanation, but how much dare he tell her?

"The brooch is unique and priceless. The gems are believed to have once been part of Empress Elizabeth's crown. The Tzar gave it to Edgemont to protect and bring to Britain."

"Protect? Why?"

It was a simple question, but he hesitated.

"Your Grace, you are too clever not to know the answer."

"And you," he paused for time to think, "are too clever to allow me not to give you one."

She gave him a smile that said he was correct.

"The value of the pin goes beyond the gems. It's one of the royal jewels."

"And?" She waited. "Edgemont didn't deal in gems. Why give it to him? The Tzar could have given it to the British Ambassador, Lord Cathcart. I'm sure the Tzar had faith in him. At least that was what he told me when he put me in Lord Cathcart's hands to return to London."

"Patrice. You must trust me."

Patrice got up and stood in front of him. Her stare was colder than their trek from the lodge.

"I've heard those words or something close to them more than once. Each time I have trusted them I came away regretting not listening to my heart. So no, Your Grace. I will not trust you with an explanation."

He stopped his hand from running through his hair. He needed to stay calm and make her understand the precarious situation they were in.

"The knowledge I have has not been confirmed. The only

people who knew the truth were Benedict Edgemont and Mr. Peters. Neither is alive, so they cannot attest to the truth of the matter.

"How convenient." Her icy stare didn't change.

He was going to have to choose his words carefully, enough for her to trust him, but not enough to get her killed.

"I do not think you are a thief on your own mission, but I do think you would gladly take the brooch for someone else." She paused. "I want to know the name of that someone else?"

Nikolai admired the way she trapped him. He finished his brandy and put his glass down. He had underestimated her when he met her in Russia and now again in Sommer-by-the-Sea.

"Not give it to someone. Prevent someone from taking it. To answer your question, I need to find the men who killed Peters to get you your answer."

He took a step and closed the space between them. He didn't take her into his arms, but he held her just the same with his eyes and his voice. "That is the only way I can keep you safe."

His words hung in the air as she understood the gravity. He accepted the victory and wanted to move on to more personal matters. His smile, the one that made her heart pound, reached his eyes. Her body betrayed her as the rush of heat spread up her neck onto her cheeks. Neither of them said anything.

"I think you're well intended," she said, "but—"

A loud knock on the front door interrupted them.

"Who the devil could that be in this storm?" Nikolai muttered.

# CHAPTER TWELVE

"**I** WON'T ANSWER it." A wave of panic was in Patrice's voice.

"That won't do. What if it is your lost boy, Henry?"

Could it be Henry? Blinking, she released him from her gaze and stepped to the window. Opening the shutters and peeking through the sheer curtain she let out a sigh.

"It's Barrington." She turned to him, "and the magistrate. I forgot they were coming here."

"I'll go to the kitchen. I won't compromise you."

"No, not there. This way." She led him to the far wall and pressed a spot on the wood molding. The jib-door opened to the servants' passageway. He nodded, stepped inside, and pulled the door shut.

She walked to the door, straightening her clothes, and opened the door.

"Barrington." She observed his raised hand, which was ready to knock again.

He stared at her and arched one eyebrow.

"Rogers, wait with the horses."

Patrice gave way as he entered the foyer.

"Have you had any luck finding Henry?" she asked following him into the parlor.

"Not yet." Barrington gave her an unnerving stare. "Who is with you?"

Here was her moment. *Tell him*, the voice inside her head said. Tell him you found a Russian prince playing the part of a vagabond in the lodge and your former solicitor dead in the maze pavilion. Instead, her heart thundered and drowned out that voice as she stood in front of Barrington who was saying something, while she was speechless. God help her.

"Lady Patrice, are you all right? You haven't heard a thing I've said."

"Please forgive me. I was thinking if there was any other place we should look for Henry."

"There are a few more houses along the cliff. I don't like leaving you alone so far from others especially in this weather. Before I leave the area I'll come to see you. If the weather worsens I will not give you the option of staying but take you to Lady Marianna at Ravencroft."

"I'm sure that won't be necessary," she said. "I have a warm fire and Tanya sent me home with food."

He looked at her intently as if judging her words. As he turned to leave, something caught his attention.

She followed his gaze to the table by the hearth where two brandy glasses remained. His face morphed from benign to concern.

"I didn't need to see the glasses to know you are not alone. You have the nicest blush."

Her cheeks got even warmer, if that were possible. She should have known the man would be perceptive.

"I ask that you be discreet."

"You have my word, as a gentleman. It is why Rogers was condemned to wait with the horses." He bowed at his words and headed for the front door.

She noticed red stains on his greatcoat. A lick of fear raced up her spine.

"I thank you for that. I went through the house and the lodge. I found no signs of Henry anywhere." Her eyes never left the stains on his coat.

He looked down at what had caught her interest.

"I noticed that the garden gate was damaged, the ground bloody."

"Yes, I went out that way when I went to see if the boy was in the lodge. I assumed it was the boar you mentioned."

He nodded. "There's nothing worse than a wounded animal. For your safety, stay inside. I'd have a hard time telling Mrs. Bainbridge I didn't take care of you. She has me sworn to come to the aid of any of you young ladies."

Did Barrington venture into the garden? The maze? Was Barrington the dutiful retired soldier that protected the village, or could he be involved with Peters? She took a deep breath to calm her growing concern.

How absurd. Now everywhere she looked she imagined duplicity. Not everyone was a villain; she just wanted to be able to sort out the ones that were, like she did rogues that frequented Almack's.

"Rogers," he called to the magistrate as he mounted his horse. "We've bothered Lady Edgemont enough. You need to go back into the village. Let Lord Percy know the boy has not been found but we are still looking. I'll stop and see Lord Manning. His estate isn't far."

"Please do be careful, Lady Edgemont," Rogers said. "There are criminals in the area. One man has already been killed."

"That will be enough, Rogers. No need to frighten Lady Edgemont," Barrington said dismissing the magistrate.

Rogers turned his horse and headed down the drive.

"Patrice."

She looked up at Barrington.

"I'll return when I'm done with Lord Manning. Now go. I'll wait until you're inside and lock the door. Do not open it for anyone but me."

Patrice didn't say anything. Rogers was already halfway down the drive. The sky had darkened. The wind gusting once again.

Barrington hadn't moved. She went inside, closed and bolted

the door, then leaned her back against it for several minutes.

She didn't care what Barrington thought of her, not really. It was Rogers' comments that bothered her.

The magistrate wasn't talking about Peters when he mentioned a murder. What was Nikolai involved in?

*Fool.*

*Men cannot be trusted.* Hadn't she learned her lesson? She made her way back into the parlor, picked up her brandy, and finished it. Was Nikolai's attention all part of a deceptive plan?

Nikolai came in through the jib-door. One glance at him and her resolve began to melt.

"Patrice."

She blinked. Nikolai stood in front of her, his face a mask of concern.

"Did Barrington upset you?"

"No. Not at all. He said he had to speak to Lord Manning immediately."

"I must leave." He looked out the window.

"No. You can't," she said and grabbed his arms. "What haven't you told me? And don't say you've told me everything."

He stared at her long and hard. What was going on in his mind? There were moments she thought she saw hurt, and something else, remorse?

"I am not as I appear, but you have deduced that. For your own safety I cannot tell you more. As soon as this is over I will."

"This? What is this?" She shoved him away and stormed to the hearth, her arms crossed over her chest.

"The people who killed Peters will stop at nothing. I'm sure they chose The Mooring for their rendezvous because they thought it would be abandoned. I'm still no closer to why Peters had the brooch with him. But I'm certain it wasn't to be found by you."

He waited a heartbeat for that to sink in. As it did, her face was a mass of emotions.

"Who?" was the only word she managed to get out.

"I thought I knew, but at the moment, I have my doubts."

Who else would come here? She glanced out the window. Barrington was out and about. He was down by the back gate and had blood on his coat. Her mind was going down a path that was horrifying. Barrington couldn't be involved, he was too trustworthy, honored. She ascribed the same qualities to Edgemont, but she had been very wrong about him.

Barrington's deception would be cruel not only to her, but also to many others. She'd known the man since they were children. But as Nikolai said, things weren't always as they appear.

Barrington told her not to venture out. Was he giving her a warning? And not about a wild boar. And like the footprints in the snow, there were two of them, him, and the magistrate.

At least Nikolai was safe with her here.

He walked over to where they had put their coats.

"Where are you going?" she said, a bit of hysterics in her voice.

"I must find—"

"No," she interrupted. "You're… you're wounded."

"I had a fine nurse and something hearty to eat. I assure you I am fine. If I am to encounter them, it will be on my terms, not theirs." He glanced toward the door. "I must find and stop them before they find us."

"You can't go out there?"

"Why?" he asked as he put on the coat.

"You don't know the area." She grabbed her coat. "I'll go with you."

"No," he said taking the coat out of her hands. "You will stay here where you'll be safe. Lock the door when I leave and don't open it for anyone. Only me."

# CHAPTER THIRTEEN

PATRICE WAS NO closer to understanding what was happening. Nikolai and Barrington weren't telling her everything. The last thing she wanted was for them to come across each other. Everything about Nikolai screamed his mind was made up. What would he do if he came upon Barrington? She had to prevent them from meeting.

"There is another way to leave the house. One where you will not be seen." Patrice stood between him and the foyer.

"I'm listening." He gave her a questioning look.

"Come with me." They went down to the ground floor. She went to the rack of keys outside the servants' hall and removed one that had an ornate tassel then led him to the end of the hallway.

"This is the wine cellar. We can go through here to the icehouse." She unlocked the door. "When I was younger, I used to help harvest the ice from the well in the summer. The ramp down the side was slick and I would slide down on a piece of carpet or a lid from one of the barrels. I'm not sure which I enjoyed more, sliding down the ramp or the challenge of climbing up the brick wall. It was easy once you knew the pattern of the bricks."

"Not something a future lady of society would do." His smile was genuine and sweet.

"Oh, no. I was scolded regularly. Playing in the icehouse was just one of my offenses."

"Why am I not surprised." He was interested in the other route and that was enough for her.

"I stopped when a piece of the ramp crumbled."

"Why do I find that hard to believe?"

"So did my father." Patrice laughed and stepped into the room. Nikolai hung back. Glancing over her shoulder to see what held him up, she was surprised to see him measuring her, for a moment she saw a pensive shimmer in the shadow of his eyes.

"What's the difference if my footprints are in the front of the house or at the back? Either way they can be followed."

"The icehouse is at the edge of the forest, yards away from the house and on the other side of the garden wall close to the river."

He gave her a non-descript nod and waited. Finally, he stepped into the wine cellar.

The windowless room had two walls lined with shelves filled with dusty bottles laying on their side. Crates were stacked two high creating waist high walls dividing the area into sections. Several bottles, spirits, no good wine connoisseur would leave wine upright, stood on the top of the crate wall as if ready to be taken to the dining room upstairs.

"Edgemont had some of the finest wines. Mr. Regis is adamant about keeping them organized. He keeps a tally on the stock and gave each variety a location number, an address if you will. He says it makes it easier and quicker to locate any bottle."

They crossed the room weaving their way around Mr. Regis' addresses to the far end of the room. Patrice opened the door. They entered a small vestibule with halls leading in two directions and a flight of stairs.

"The stairs lead to the servants' entrance to the library and billiard room. The hall on the right goes to the storage rooms, the one on the left to the icehouse.

They went to the left. A short way down the hall they came

to a door. To the side were three empty wheelbarrows. Pike poles, some missing heads, leaned against the wall. Scarves and gloves hung from a row of pegs.

"I played here so often my father had a lock installed. Ah, but I found the secret."

Her hand slid across the top of the door frame and grabbed the key. Without facing him she hesitated. "The magistrate said someone was murdered. He doesn't know about Mr. Peters in the maze."

Nikolai bowed his head. She glanced at him from the corner of her eyes. Even she could see he was weighing his answer.

"If you are asking me if I killed someone, the answer is no. I was with the man when we were attacked. He saved my life. I wish I could have saved his."

She didn't say anything and turned the key. She wanted to believe him. The door opened easily.

He stared into darkness.

"It's a well-traveled tunnel with a stone floor." She handed him the lantern. "Take the key. You'll need it to open the door on the other side. When you leave the icehouse, the stream will be to your right. Follow it for four miles. It isn't the quickest route to the road, but it is the easiest in this weather. It will take you through the forest and behind the trees in front of the house. If it's your intent to go to the road, cross a meadow and you'll come to an outcropping. There is a small cave there where you can rest if it isn't filled with snow. From there, it won't be much further to the road."

She pulled a green scarf off one of the pegs. "Will I see you later?" she asked as she wrapped it around his neck.

He didn't answer. He sniffed the scarf. "Lavender."

Her hands froze for a moment before she continued.

"Mother didn't want the ice to smell like hay. She had lavender planted around the mound and spread on the icehouse floor. The fragrance permeated everything."

"I would know the scent anywhere. It tickles my nose."

"I could find you another." She began to unwrap the wool.

"I actually enjoy the fragrance. It's soft and subtly sweet." He stilled her hands then released them.

"Where will you go?" Her hands fell to her side once she was done fashioning the scarf.

"It's best I don't tell you."

"Because of the Tzar? Some great secret."

From the glare he gave her, the playful, gallant gentleman was gone. At the moment, she didn't care.

"I don't want to argue." He held her by her shoulders. "I won't put you in jeopardy. These aren't young dandies playing a game. These are very ruthless men. There is too much at stake that I cannot disclose. I promise that I will tell you everything. Just not now."

More than anything, Patrice wanted to believe him.

"Be careful." Reluctantly, she stepped away from him. "There are traps and snares well hidden in the forest."

"You needn't worry. I have hiked and hunted in the mountains all my life. I will be careful."

He stared at her as if he was memorizing her features. She didn't need to do the same. Patrice knew every feature of his face down to his smile, which was as intimate as a kiss.

Nikolai turned, walked through the door, and began to pull it closed. Then he stopped.

"I will be back, and when I have returned, it will be as the Grand Duke, not a vagabond."

He stepped into the tunnel and closed the door before she could say a word.

Patrice stood unable to move, staring at the door, listening to the sound of his retreating footsteps. When they faded into nothingness she hurried up the stairs and through the house to the nursery.

She threw open the door and rushed to the window and waited. The snow was a solid white curtain, falling fast. She wiped the window clean as best she could for a better view. The maze didn't draw her attention. With her fingers drumming on the windowsill and her face practically against the windowpane, she focused her attention on the lone building at the edge of the forest.

It didn't take long before she saw a blur of movement near the icehouse. With the thick snow falling and the wind gusting, she could barely make out the smudge of green among all the white.

She stared out the window into the emptiness. Restless and irritable, she pounded her fist on the windowsill. This was getting her nowhere.

Did she do the right thing, directing him away from Barrington?

Patrice took a deep breath as she left the room and went back to the parlor. She picked up the brandy glasses and headed down to the scullery. As she passed the servants' hall she saw that his empty soup bowl was still on the table, along with his half-eaten piece of bread and the brooch.

She stared at the brooch then tucked the gem into her pocket. Sinking into the chair, the one he had occupied, she tried to piece together what happened earlier. Did he need the brooch? What if he was caught and ordered to hand it over? Would they beat him? With his wound, he wouldn't survive.

Her head told her to be patient. He said to stay inside.

Her heart told her to help him.

*"Take time to deliberate, but when the time for action has arrived, stop thinking and go."*

Patrice hurried into the parlor and stood at the window. The snow had lightened. She grabbed her coat and put it on as she went down into the kitchen. She stuffed her hair under her red cap and pulled on her gloves. She went out the garden door and walked along the outer edges of the maze to the back gate. On the other side, she found traces from Barrington and the horses. He *had* been here.

It wasn't any desire for more information. It wasn't out of

duty. It wasn't out of anything, other than her heart told her to go after him. Help him. With renewed purpose, she headed toward the road.

# Chapter Fourteen

THE TUNNEL INCLINE rose as Nikolai made his way to the part of the icehouse that was above ground. At last he entered the brick lined room. There was little there except the ice harvesting tools, several ice saws, tongs, gaffs, and picks.

He peered into the deep ice well and wasn't surprised to find blocks of ice remained at the bottom. Before he went into the woods, he needed some form of protection. He wished he had his knife, but he had lost that at Philby's.

He looked at the wall of tools and hefted the gaff. Too cumbersome and heavy. He chose one of the smaller picks.

Once he was outside he admired the construction of the small building. Secluded as it was among the trees and undergrowth, it was well disguised. The recessed door of the man-made mound faced north and for this storm was protected to some degree from the snow drifts. He covered his tracks as best he could, not wanting to lead anyone to the remote building, then followed the river.

He pulled the coat collar over the green scarf and stuffed the rest inside his coat. The last thing he wanted was for someone to easily spot him.

He should never have encouraged her or let himself get close to Patrice. He did neither of them any favors. She was every bit as intelligent and beautiful as he remembered. If things had been different, he could have saved her from the heartache of these two years.

Would she consider his delay another deception? Well, that couldn't be helped. There was more at stake than the woman's feelings. If she didn't forgive him, at least she would know the truth about Edgemont. Thanks to Philby. At least that part of his mission would be a success.

By his estimation, he was halfway to the road. So far nothing was out of place. The only tracks he came across was the occasional small animal. He moved on through the eerie, muted stillness keeping watch for Barrington and anyone else.

The snap of a branch broke through the stillness. His heart pounded. In the muffled air it was difficult to identify the sound's direction. He gripped the ice pick defensively and moved on. He knew someone was near, but did they know where he was? He kept moving.

He left the forest as the river made its way through the open field. The outcropping was ahead. It was urgent that he give his contact a quick briefing regarding Mr. Peters as well as his current situation. Once he completed that, there was a good chance he would be sent back to St. Petersburg. If Patrice could be brought into their confidence, he would tell her all she wanted to know.

Bombarded by ice and wind, he hunkered down as he began to cross the field. The weather was brutal. His legs were like weights and his side was beginning to ache, but like he was on a forced march, Nikolai kept moving.

He came to the large outcropping. A quick glance ahead and he saw the cave opening. His beard iced over, he looked forward to getting into the cave and out of the wind. His head down, he moved on and stepped inside.

"Ah, Nikolai. So glad you could join us."

Nikolai stared at Sergei Lazovsky. Patrice stood next to him. His heart sank. He thought she was safe when here she was in the hands of a man who was paid to intimidate and torture.

He never worked without Yuri Sivnikov. Nikolai wondered

where *he* was.

"Sergei. Yuri isn't with you? I thought I saw your work earlier. Did Peters give you what you wanted?"

"Did *Peters* give us?" He looked from Patrice to him. "Ah, I see what you're doing. Did you tell this lovely lady that we spoke with Peters? You did. And she believed you?"

"It doesn't really matter what you claim." Patrice's imperious voice brought both men to full attention. "You are a clumsy assassin. He was still alive when we found him. He whispered his last words in my ear."

Nikolai stared at her. She hadn't come close to Peters' body. What was she doing? Before he could stop her, she continued.

"Sergei and Yuri, he told me. 'I wouldn't talk no matter what they did,' he said. So you see, I know exactly who tortured and killed Mr. Peters."

Sergei grabbed Patrice and held her in front of him.

"If you want her to live you'll—"

"You'll what?" Patrice stomped on his foot. Before he could respond, Patrice was behind him, kicking him in the back of his knees, which brought the man to the ground.

Nikolai, his hands clasped like a sledgehammer, swung at Sergei, hitting him in the jaw.

The man's head flew back. Blood sprayed from his nose, dusting Sergei's cheeks like a spray of red freckles. He stared, his eyes rolling up before he fell backwards and was out.

A large hand landed on Nikolai's shoulder and yanked him around.

"No!" Patrice screamed.

Nikolai twisted his head, looking for her.

A swift punch caught him in his side. He doubled over in pain and his chin got in the way of an upper cut.

He lifted his head and tried to focus, but everything was a blur. With great effort he made out Sergei moving, and Yuri restraining Patrice, who hollered and tried to reach him.

Her screams faded. His heart pounded. Everything spun

around him. He reached for Patrice, but all he got was empty air for his efforts.

Hauled onto someone's back, he fought to stay in the moment, be aware of where Patrice was and who had her. But he was unable to keep his thoughts together. In a final effort, he lifted his head and saw Sergei pushing Patrice along in front of him. He saw Patrice's brave smile before everything went black.

He was coming around when he was ceremoniously dropped on a floor. Patrice's muffled voice tried to get through to him.

As his senses came back, he woke to the aroma of lavender. The icehouse. He tried to move, but his body wouldn't respond.

A rough hand grabbed his shoulder, pulling him onto his back.

"Not yet, Yuri. I am a sentimental man. Let his lover say good-bye. Then you can push him into the well. No one will miss a vagabond. Many in the village will think Lady Edgemont a great heroine. With her last ounce of energy, ridding them of such a person."

Patrice bent over him and whispered in his ear. Only snippets of what she said made it through the fog. Desperate words from the tone of her voice. *Follow the wall. Hold. Hand. Access. Doors. Secret.* And a jumble of other words he couldn't decipher.

Fighting to stay in the moment, he gave up trying to open his eyes or make sense of what she said.

She kissed his lips. He opened his eyes enough to see pain etched in her face. Her mouth was moving but all he heard was his drumming heartbeat in his head.

His eyes closed as he rolled over. Then the sickening feeling of rushing down a hill overtook him. A jolt. A crash. Then everything went black.

HE WOKE ON his stomach, his face numb and cold. He planted his hands down to push up and became wide awake. Ice. He blinked to focus but was unable to see anything in the inky blackness. There was no wind, no snow. Nothing.

He'd been cold before, colder than now when he was in Moscow following the French occupation. Napoleon marched into the city to find it abandoned and ablaze. Nikolai and his men did a good job, but they weren't through. They were determined to rout out the invaders from their beloved city. They'd killed them any way they could, murder or starvation. It didn't matter.

For weeks he lived alone in the darkness in the Domodedovo caves an hour from Moscow as the Frenchman hunted him. No light, little warmth, and hardly any food. But he outsmarted the French commander, Napoleon's henchman.

Nikolai celebrated when he heard of the man's death at the hands of the British. His only regret was he wasn't with the detail that killed him.

Reliving that time wasn't getting him out of here. It did get his blood moving enough to clear his mind. He pushed away all thoughts of Moscow. He needed to get out of wherever he was.

*Breathe. That's it.*

His nose twitched. Lavender. Yes, yes, now he remembered. He was in the icehouse.

He flexed his arms and legs. Nothing was broken, only badly bruised. He sat up in the darkness to get his bearings and stretched out his arms. His hand banged against a brick wall. He looked up but he couldn't see anything.

While he waited for his eyes to adjust to the dark, his senses took over. The silence was deafening. The ground was cold to his touch, strewn with ice and large fragments of wood.

The sensation of sliding lingered around the edges of his mind. As the image came into focus he remembered one minute, sliding down an incline, and the next, crashing and tumbling. He had no recollection of anything else.

Little by little, his eyes adjusted to the shades of black and grey. He looked up and barely made out the top edge of the wall thirty feet above him. He didn't have to search the ice well to know he was alone.

He grimaced at the pounding in his head and stabbing pain in his side. It was senseless to try and get to his feet. He forced his mind off his discomfort and concentrated on trying to piece things together.

Patrice's voice kept buzzing in his head.

*"You must remember… Follow…."*

Follow who? what?

"Follow… Follow…" he repeated over and over waiting for the additional words to fall into place.

"The wall." His head snapped to the right. His foggy mind was clearing. "Follow the wall."

He reached toward the wall and slowly got to his feet.

*Stay calm. Save your strength.*

He slid his hand along the wall to follow it to the top. If he kept close to the stones and went slowly, he was sure he could get out of the well. He needed to be careful. Somewhere up ahead the ramp had collapsed. He had no idea how big the break was or how he would cross it. He'd find out soon enough.

With a painstaking effort he continued up the ramp, testing each step as he went. Time passed slowly, but he kept going. Every minute he wasted was another minute Patrice was in danger.

He kept his hands running along the wall and as his head stopped throbbing, he quickened his pace. Thoughts of what he'd do to Sergei and Yuri urged him on.

He was into a routine, stretching and grasping onto the stone wall and testing the ground. Setting his foot down and repeating the process.

He thought Peters' murder was Sergei and Yuri's work. Who had sent them to Sommer-by-the-Sea? Instead of testing the ground, he put his foot down and found nothing beneath it. His mind snapped back to what he was doing.

He grabbed for the stone outcroppings on the well wall, but

his hands slipped off the stone and he found himself sliding.

He fought to find a hand hold, any hand hold. One after another slipped past him until finally, he was able to grab one and hold on. His feet scrambled until they too found an outcropping.

He clung to the wall. He was thankful the walls of the well were a cone and not straight or else he would have landed back on top of the ice. His heart pounded as he struggled to find the next foot hold. He cursed himself for his lack of attention. Without any idea of how far he fell or how close he might be to the ramp, his only option was to climb straight up the wall.

His arms ached from the strain. His energy waning, he didn't stop. His feet felt for the next crevice, then his hand reached for a higher hand hold. He kept going, his mind focused solely on climbing up the wall.

His side burned, but he kept moving.

He reached for the next hand hold and instead, he felt the edge of the well.

"At last." He wasn't out of the well yet. He heaved himself as high as possible, threw his leg over the side, and then rolled onto the icehouse floor.

His clothes were damp with sweat, his arms were heavy, his breathing labored. Spent, he rested and gathered his strength.

The lavender's fragrance was stronger here. He took deep gulps of air as his heart rate returned to something near normal. Sensation was back in his arms. From his vantage point, he could see light and a small dusting of snow coming in under the outside door.

On his feet, he staggered to the way out. With each step he was more determined to find Patrice and her abductors. He knew what these men were capable of.

He tugged the coat around himself and wrapped the scarf around his neck. Ready to go on, he tried the latch. Locked. He slammed his hand against the door. Even if he had an axe, the blasted thing was so thick he wouldn't be able to get through it.

Leaning his head against the door, he closed his eyes. He had failed. Worse, he had failed Patrice.

Her voice echoed in his head. Her soft words. *Secret.*

Nikolai froze. *You know the secret.* He moved away from the door. A flash of recognition hit him. *The key is the secret.*

He patted his pocket, but it wasn't there. He ran his hand on the frame above the door. He was almost all the way across. Nothing. He went to the very end before he felt the cold metal.

Carefully, Nikolai put the key into the lock and turned. A loud click set him free. Engaging the latch, he swung the door open letting in the light. He looked at his prison one last time and was about to step out when he stopped.

Where would they take Patrice? Not into the village. They would take her to get the brooch, back to the house.

He looked across at the door to the tunnel. It would be quicker, and he would be unnoticed if he went in that way.

He closed the outside door, went across the room, and un-locked the tunnel door. Once inside he closed and locked the icehouse door behind him.

He made his way to the wine cellar door. The room would be difficult to cross without any light. The butler's system made the place an obstacle course. He picked through the pike poles that were against the wall until he found one he liked.

His body tingled with energy. He needed to tame his eager-ness. He would be no use to Patrice or himself if he was brash. Not with these thugs. Hefting the pole, he opened the wine cellar door.

Mumbled curses fell from his lips, admonishing himself. He should have been more observant when he went through the room earlier. The path across the room wasn't necessarily difficult. The door to the other side was directly across the room. It was the bottles on the crates that concerned him. Any one of them falling could set off a warning.

He fixed his goal in his mind, closed the door, and stood with his back against it. The crates and bottles were there, but even as he strained to make out what he was about to encounter, he couldn't see anything.

He held the pole centered in front of him and dragged it over the brick floor, first to his left then to his right in an arc not much wider than his body. One step. No obstacle.

Slowly swinging the pole in a gentle arc, he progressed across the room.

He had gone ten paces when the pole struck a crate. Concentrating on his steps and moving his pole, he altered his path as necessary.

His instinct said he was headed in the correct direction, but he should have been at the door by now. He could feel the closeness of the wall. It couldn't be much further now.

Where would Sergei and Yuri take Patrice? The library? Edgemont's room? He didn't know the house well. It would take him time to navigate. His earlier search with Patrice proved the layout was somewhat predictable, but not completely. If Sergei and Yuri were looking for documents, the best place to start would be—

A raised brick on the floor tripped him. He stumbled off balance into one of the crates. The bottles clinked together.

He heard more than saw one bottle rolling. Pictures of a catastrophe flashed in his mind, a bottle rolling into others bringing them down like tenpins and crashing on the floor.

He focused all his energy on the top of the crate and barely made out the shapes of the dark bottles. The movement was enough to give him a hint of their outline. He reached out with his right hand and caught the bottle as it rolled over the side.

He stood holding the pike and the bottle, unable to move. After his heart calmed down, he tucked the bottle in his coat pocket and continued. Two more steps and he reached the wall.

His hands trembled as he ran them across the wall searching for the door. With luck, he was going in the correct direction. Four more steps and if he didn't find the way out, he'd turn to go the other way. He reached his hand out and felt the coolness of the metal hinge.

He continued until he reached the latch. With renewed determination, he tried the door. It wasn't locked.

Squinting, he opened the door a crack, letting his eyes adjust to the light. After a few heartbeats, he opened it wider and looked about. No one was there. Relieved, he stepped out. He leaned the pike against the wall inside the wine cellar and closed it behind him. The area was dimly lit. He glanced up the stairwell. There were four landings and at the top the large skylight.

He stood silently by the steps to get his bearings and listened for any indication of where Patrice might be. They would most likely take her to Edgemont's library, or at least that was where he would start. The staircase that faced him led to the billiard room. He wondered if there was also a passageway to the library.

Silently, he started up the stairs. No one would be expecting him and that was his greatest advantage. On the first landing were two green baize panels, jib-doors, with hook and eye locks. Pressing his ear to the adjacent wall, he heard the muffled sound of voices.

He listened at the next room. Nothing. He pushed that door open. He peeked in and found comfortable chairs and the billiard table. With the room empty, he went inside.

The cue rack was on the wall adjacent to the library. Carefully, he examined the wood paneled wall and found the outline of another jib-door. Muffled voices came from the other side. He put his ear to the wall.

"Don't be upset. Nikolai has fooled many people with his aristocratic ways." Sergei was never his biggest supporter.

"He's a killer with a gilded tongue. You're not the only person he's fooled." Yuri followed Sergei. He never did have an independent thought or idea.

"What makes you think he's fooled me?"

A cold sweat broke out across Nikolai's forehead. On one hand, he was relieved he had found her. On the other hand, Patrice was an intelligent woman, but she had no idea how to deal with these men. He stayed where he was and listened, his mind working for the best way to get Patrice away from them.

"I am aware of who and what he is. I have my own reasons for befriending him."

He rolled with his back against the wall.

*No, Patrice. You have no idea how to play this game.*

CHAPTER FIFTEEN

PATRICE WORKED HARD not to fidget as she sat in the library. The door to the wall safe stood open. The men were excited, at least Yuri was, when she opened it. She had no idea what they expected to find. Rubles? Did they think she was that dense not to have emptied the safe long ago?

No, it was a game. They wanted the safe opened but made no demands when they found it was empty. It wasn't money or papers they wanted. No, they sat across from her drinking Edgemont's brandy and waited for something or someone.

She had already taken Sergei and Yuri to Edgemont's bedroom. They didn't believe her when she told them they would find nothing. She had his room emptied and things tossed out when she returned to The Mooring after his funeral.

Her mother had been irate that she mourned for less than two months, but even that was too long as far as she was concerned. Who ever heard of a wife mourning for an unfaithful husband? No, she couldn't toss his things out fast enough to rid herself of his stench.

In the quiet of the room, the library clock chimed the hour.

And Nikolai. As soon as they dropped him on the icehouse floor, she knew they intended to toss him into the well.

She had to think fast when they told her to roll him over the edge. It was only by chance that they dropped him by the wooden plank close to the ramp and let her say her last words to him.

They didn't give her much time. What little they gave her she spent trying to give him instructions, but there was no recognition in his eyes. With all her heart she hoped Nikolai had understood her words.

When Sergei stepped toward her, she shoved the board with Nikolai on it down the ramp rather than letting them throw him over the side. It was the best she could do at the time. It was the *only* thing she could do.

Sergei was irate until he heard the wood plank hit the stone wall and splinter into a thousand pieces. That was when he finally moved her outside and pushed her towards the house.

Yuri, his glass empty, poured the last drop of brandy into his glass.

"Got any more?" He held up his glass.

"If there is more, it would be in the wine cellar." The last thing she wanted was to bring them there and possibly find Nikolai.

Sergei gave Yuri a wicked look then relented and turned to her without saying a word.

"Is that your way of requesting more brandy?" Her icy glare made him scowl.

The man was beginning to show signs of losing his patience. Rather than get him angry and require an escort, she got to her feet and took one of the lit lanterns.

"Go with her." Sergei gestured to Yuri as she closed the library door.

"And where is she going to go?" That was the last thing she heard from Yuri as she hurried along. Let the two of them work it out. The easiest thing to do was get below stairs before either of them followed. They wouldn't know where to go by themselves.

She ran down the staircase in the vestibule and hurried past the footman's rooms to the wine cellar.

Patrice opened the latch. Without another thought, she

rushed inside, immediately closed the door behind her, and hung the lantern on a peg.

"Do you think he followed you?"

A smile bloomed on her face. His low mellow tone was music to her ears. Tension that had built up over the last several hours drained, leaving her spent as she whipped around to face him.

"I don't think so," she whispered. "I left them—"

"Arguing whether you needed an escort," he interrupted. "I listened from the billiard room. I found the jib-door."

He took her into his arms and held her close.

"I had to slide you down the ramp. I was concerned—"

"Hush. You did what needed to be done. We're safe here for a while, but sooner or later they will begin to look for you."

"I think they're waiting for someone." She enjoyed his warmth and snuggled closer. "I don't know who it could be…"

He pulled away and stared at her.

"What?" she asked.

"They're waiting for Peters." He lowered his head. "I have an uncomfortable feeling that someone else may have killed him. Someone who didn't know he had your brooch."

"Mr. Peters was an opportunist. I didn't say anything until he made some remarks about Edgemont. Then I took care of him quite nicely. So nicely, he was forced to leave for the continent. The man wasn't very happy. As a matter of fact, he threatened me before he left."

"Whomever killed him did you a favor, but that was not his intent. Peters must have gotten someone other than Sergei and Yuri angry. But who and over what?"

"Let me get a bottle of brandy and bring it to them. They're not going to go away because I didn't return."

"I'm not happy about that."

She reached up and kissed his lips.

"I'll be careful. I'll think of something that will make them leave." She searched the top of one of the crates.

"Tell them you're expecting Barrington. That will make them

move."

"Barrington? Why on earth would his name scare them off?"

"His reputation precedes him even in Russia."

"Ah. I would take up two bottles but there is only one here."

He took the bottle out of his pocket and handed it to an amazed Patrice.

"It's a long story. Suffice it to say, I saved it from a disastrous end for both the bottle and for me."

"I'll tell them Barrington is expected. What will you do?"

"I'll be in the billiard room. I won't be far from you."

"When this is settled, you have to tell me the long story about the nearly disastrous end of the brandy." With the bottles in hand, she took the lantern.

"It will be my pleasure." Nikolai opened the door and they both left.

He headed for the servants' stairs.

She went down the passageway and up the stairs to the ground level and entered the library.

"Two bottles," Yuri exclaimed, a broad smile on his face.

"Yes, with Barrington and his men coming shortly, I thought it best to bring one up for them as well."

Sergei and Yuri looked at each other. The look on their faces would have been comical if the situation wasn't so serious.

She turned to the clock then back at them. "Within the next half-hour or so. Do you know His Lordship?"

Sergei grabbed her arm and pulled her toward him.

"You play a very dangerous game, Lady Edgemont."

He was hurting her, but she was determined not to let him know.

"You two have no idea what you have brought upon yourselves. No idea at all." She tugged her arm away from him, opened the brandy and poured herself a glass then took a seat by the hearth.

"We'll see who plays a dangerous game," she said, as she sat there sipping.

# CHAPTER SIXTEEN

PATRICE GLANCED AT Sergei. His attitude was totally different from Yuri's. Yuri was the more agreeable of the two.

Sergei had an angry jeer etched on his lips. Hateful would best describe him, but there was an element of something else she couldn't quite place. He filled his glass with brandy and for a moment, before he took a drink, his mask faltered and she saw what he'd been hiding, fear, stark and naked.

The reactions of both men amazed her. Reese Barrington was clever and elegant and had a commanding presence. She found it sweet the way he and Mrs. Bainbridge interacted. As if the headmistress could hide her attraction. Come to think of it, neither could Barrington. It made it even more difficult to see him as a threat the way these men did.

"We should leave before Barrington and his men get here." Yuri was now in perpetual motion. When he wasn't bouncing from one foot to the other, he was pacing between the window and the hearth, hands in and out of his pockets.

Barrington was revered by the men he served as well as the men he led. Even retired, he commanded respect. The man was busy with visits from former officers and soldiers as well as an abundance of government people, which didn't come as a surprise. Barrington's brother Lord Edward was in the House of Lords.

Lord Edward's skills went beyond political strategy and negotiation. Without a militia in Sommer-by-the-Sea, he often called upon Reese and his friends for assistance.

Sergei and Yuri were on the other side of the room in a heated argument. She was not proficient in Russian and only understood every third or fourth word, enough to realize they were trying to decide what to do. They'd tell her soon enough.

Patrice took another sip of brandy. She came home to The Mooring to see if young Henry was here and found herself deep in some sinister plot. What was this puzzle? Russian thugs were after Nikolai, and he hid from Barrington. Somehow, in the middle of this mess was Edgemont, their visit to Russia, the Royal Brooch, and a very dead Joseph Peters.

Her coat landed in her lap. Her head flew up and she stared at Sergei, his coat on, standing in front of her. She glanced at Yuri. He too was dressed to go outside.

"Put it on."

When she hesitated, he grabbed her arm and pulled her to her feet.

"I won't tell you again. Put on the coat or go outside without it. It's up to you." He pushed her away from him.

The thought of going outside as she was dressed was enough to convince her to follow his orders. Patrice shrugged into her coat.

"What will happen when he arrives?" Yuri stuffed his hands in his coat pockets and stared at Sergei, a blank expression on his face.

"He'll have to sit and wait." Sergei shrugged his shoulders. "He can explain to Barrington why he's here."

"But what if he—" In two strides Sergei was in front of Yuri.

"Shut up, you fool." Sergei stood in Yuri's immediate vicinity, his threatening stance indeed shutting him up.

"Out," Sergei commanded as he opened the door, and pushed Yuri and Patrice forward.

NIKOLAI STOOD BEHIND the closed window shutter in the parlor staring between the louvers. Sergei, Yuri, and Patrice, wearing her red cap, made their way across the snow-covered lawn toward the forest.

He knew Barrington's name would get them moving. Patrice had done an excellent job. But waiting to see who the other players were in this game was not an option, not with Patrice at the mercy of Sergei and Yuri.

He finished her glass of brandy to dull the building pain. There wasn't time enough to wait for the brandy to take effect. Limping to the door, he took one of Edgemont's walking sticks then left the house and tracked them in the woods.

He moved as quickly as he could manage across the open space. The wind whipped around, the cold seeping through the coat. Tired and drained, he ignored the discomfort and went on. Leaning heavily on the walking stick, he did his best to stay out of sight, counting on the blizzard to hide him.

Eight yards into the woods, he stopped and knelt for a close look at the tracks.

"Bloody hell." The set of tracks he followed had changed. One of them – Yuri, he suspected – had gone off in a different direction. How had he missed it? He stood and scanned the direction the lone tracks headed.

The maneuver was one of Sergei's signature strategies. Divide and conquer. The pursuer followed Sergei while Yuri circled behind, putting whoever hunted him at a disadvantage.

They weren't expecting him or Barrington. No. They left the house to avoid Barrington. They didn't want him getting in the way of their plan. Whomever he and Yuri were meeting was their target. If it was Peters, they were in for a long wait.

The wound in his side escalated from a dull throb to a burning pain. He banished his misery into a blunt annoyance. There was no time for him to dwell on his injury. Staying alert was a necessity.

Nikolai retraced his steps until he found the place where the other tracks went off in another direction.

To his left, he caught a glimpse of a red cap bobbing on the trail ahead. The parallel tracks were far enough away for Yuri to be out of sight but within striking distance.

Yuri would have to be eliminated. Success would mean that Sergei had no one coming to his aid. His plan set, Nikolai continued.

A flurry of snow ahead caught his attention. It was Yuri wading through a thicket, sending the snow flying.

The brandy was taking effect. With his side numb and the walking stick for assistance, Nikolai moved cautiously among the trees keeping his prey in sight.

A movement to his left made him take cover behind a tree. About ten yards away he made out Patrice. She and Sergei had stopped. They stood by a waist-high stone wall. From his vantage point, she didn't appear in distress or harmed. There was no telling how much longer that would last. Knowing Sergei, his disposition could change at any moment. Nikolai had to act fast.

A glance toward Yuri found the overly confident man roosting behind a tightly knit stand of trees.

He moved to the group of tall bushes and put Yuri between himself and Sergei. He went over his few resources. He had to be creative. Creative with what? He didn't have a weapon. He stomped the hazelwood cane in front of him, sending a small cascade of snow off the low branches of the bush. He glanced at Yuri. The man watched Sergei and Patrice.

They were using Patrice as bait to draw out someone. He needed to divert Yuri's attention, lure the man away. A smile spread across his face. It wouldn't be easy, but with luck he might succeed.

Nikolai unwound the scarf from around his neck then tied one end onto the walking stick and set it on top of the hedgerow.

Staying low and out of sight, he walked and pulled the cane along the top of the bushes, sending the snow flying.

At the end of the hedgerow, Nikolai quickly freed the walking stick and worked his way behind his target.

Yuri, mumbling in Russian under his breath, came to investigate. He examined the area. Nothing. He glanced toward the tracks, but they were covered by the disturbed snow.

Annoyed, the thug turned. His jaw flapped, but no words came out.

"Predatel," Nikolai said. Traitor.

The man fumbled in his pocket.

Nikolai didn't give him time to gather his weapon. He grabbed him by his ears and as he raised his leg, smashed his head into his knee.

In a fit of frenzy, he fought in a trance-like fury. His need to protect Patrice surpassed his discomfort, his injury. Nikolai, still holding the man by the hair on the back of his head, pulled him in front of him and whispered in his ear. "That was for Leonid."

Yuri's lips trembled as horror and fright washed over his face.

"No." The word caught in his throat as he choked it out. "Sergei. It was Sergei."

"I saw you," he lied.

"How? You weren't there. Sergei told me to go ahead, you'd never find out."

"That's all I needed to know."

"You tricked me," Yuri moaned in agony. "We can go after Sergei together."

He may have tricked the confession out of Yuri, but that satisfaction was only the beginning. Nikolai's nostrils flared as the resentment he had stifled began to smolder. His blood raced through his veins as anger rolled through him until he couldn't contain his fury a moment longer.

Holding the killer by his hair, his other hand grabbed his chin. In a swift motion, he quickly twisted his head upward and to the side, lifting Yuri off the ground.

The exertion burned Nikolai's chest. He didn't stop. He wasn't finished. Forcibly, he twisted the other way. The momentum of Yuri's body did the rest.

The delicate vertebrae cracked. The weight of the victim's body should have been enough. But like a deadly animal, he gave another shake. The fury began to fade. Then Nikolai let his body slide into the snow.

As an afterthought, he reached into Yuri's pocket and withdrew a knife. It was his knife, the one he lost at Philby's.

Nikolai slashed Yuri's throat for good measure, then cleaned the blade on the dead man's coat. There was one person left that he needed to deal with, and another he needed to rescue.

He looked toward the stone wall. Her red cap was gone.

✦

# CHAPTER SEVENTEEN

WITHOUT WARNING, SERGEI hurried Patrice away from the stone wall and along the stream.

"I didn't hear anything." She turned and faced him.

He reached for her.

Her hands flew to her head.

He grabbed her red cap, pulled it off, and stuffed it into his pocket.

"Keep walking." He pushed her along as he kept a constant eye on the area.

The hair on the back of her neck stood up. Someone was watching them, and she had no idea if it was friendly eyes or not.

Now wasn't the time to be fainthearted or tentative. If she was going to take any action it had to be before Yuri, or whoever was following them, took Sergei's side.

She knew better than to bait the man. His jittering jaw muscle and flexing fists were all signs of a man tightly wound, ready to erupt.

*Be patient. Watch for the right time.*

She pulled the collar up on her coat, marched on, and assessed the area around her. It was almost like being back at the seminary trying to outwit the others.

*Stay focused. This game has deadly consequences.* They approached the stream. She stiffened. In the distance she heard the waterfall.

Without hesitating, she quickened her steps and widened the distance between herself and Sergei. He did nothing. She increased the distance even more then took off at a run.

Sergei's heavy footfalls got louder as he shortened the distance between them.

Veering off the path, she crashed through the bushes and sped past the blur of trees as she headed toward the lake.

As she approached the shore, she was pulled back by her collar mid-stride, then pushed forward with such force she fell in the snow. He was on top of her, panting hard. His breath smelled sour, not like the smokey aroma of Edgemont's brandy she was used to. Everything about the man was foul.

Sergei got to his feet and pulled her up.

Patrice tossed a handful of snow into his face, turned her back to him, and aimed to dig her elbow as hard as she could into his stomach, but he was ready for her.

Still wiping the snow from his eyes, he made a quarter turn to avoid her attack.

He looked up, his arm raised and ready to strike her, but it was Nikolai who stood in front of him with a smile that didn't reach his eyes.

"Predatel," Nikolai said, then slammed the walking stick down on Sergei's head. Blood trickled down his face.

"Go," Nikolai commanded.

She didn't move.

"Now." Nikolai pushed her away.

She bolted, speeding through the woods to the lake, and didn't look back.

NIKOLAI WAS RELIEVED she was safe. Now he would finish what was started all those years ago.

"What does it take to kill you?" Sergei asked, insinuating killing him was just an annoyance.

"Was it easier to kill your uncle and the men with him? It must have been. They trusted you. You were there to protect them." His eyes never wavered. He kept them on the traitor.

"My family served your father for decades and what did we get?"

"The family candlesticks, jewels. Yet, he kept you close. Should I go on?"

"Out of guilt," Sergei yelled. His eyes flittered from Nikolai to their surroundings.

"No, not guilt. He thought you were petty criminals, not men who would sell secrets to the enemy. Steal state papers from him and make it look like he was the traitor. He kept you close to prevent you and Yuri from being executed for treason."

"Yuri talks too much. You know you can't believe anything he says." The man shrugged off the statement. "It was nothing personal. We were told where to be and when the men came out of the palace, to kill them. We weren't told who they were, for our own protection, he said."

"Yuri corroborated what I already knew. Your mother came to me heartsick. She told me who killed my father and the others."

Sergei started to interrupt.

Nikolai put up his hand to ward him off.

"She came willingly. You killed her cousin and friend. The daughter of the Grand Duchess is still a great woman who is respected for more than just her mushroom barley soup." That brought a smile to Nikolai.

Sergei didn't move, but he scanned the area, waiting.

"Are you expecting someone? Peters is dead, you know. In the maze. Lady Edgemont found him."

Nikolai watched the emotion on Sergei's face change from smug, to anger, and finally to hate. Sergei had a temper and when riled, he was unable to control the overwhelming need to strike out. When he snapped, he was careless and most vulnerable. Nikolai waited a little longer, relaxed, calm, watching.

Sergei pulled a knife from his pocket and flashed it in front of Nikolai.

Nikolai already had his knife in his hand. He had no intention of trying to scare Sergei. He had every intention of killing him.

He blocked Sergei's attack with the back of his arm to protect the veins on the underside of his forearm. Sergei's strike left him vulnerable. Nikolai took full advantage. Still close, but unable to get to his arm, he aimed for Sergei's artery by jabbing his knife into the thug's thigh. He quickly stepped back out of striking distance.

The man stumbled and looked at the knife in Nikolai's hand.

"That's your knife. Yuri had it." He looked from the knife to Nikolai's eyes and curled his lip into an ugly sneer.

"Not anymore." Nikolai's voice was punishing, lifeless, and unemotional. "He too is dead. I would say I'm sorry, but I'm not. No, not at all. There is nothing worse than a traitor. How the French used you. You killed the only men who would protect you. Now you have no one, not even your mother."

Sergei roared and rushed him.

Even badly wounded, Sergei was a lethal threat. That left Nikolai with no room for any errors.

Sergei tackled him to the ground. "It was an education taking the jewels from Edgemont's wife. Did you know she sleeps without any clothes? Would you like to know—"

The words were knocked out of Sergei's mouth along with some of his teeth. Sergei put some distance between them. Nikolai, in full rage, had every intention of shutting the man's mouth forever.

Sergei rushed him. Nikolai closed the space between them and pushed Sergei's knife away. He punched him in the chest, each strike for a person he killed, each strike more powerful than the last.

He swiveled to his right and caught Sergei's free arm. With

precision, he dropped to his knee, brought Sergei over his back to land hard on the ground in a perfectly choreographed maneuver.

Sergei didn't stay down long. He was back on his feet and dove at him low and fast. Surprised by his quick recovery, the powerful punch knocked the knife out of Nikolai's hand.

Sergei's smug smile didn't hide his fear. It drove Nikolai on.

Like a fine ballet, Nikolai had rehearsed this final scene over and over in his head. He knew Sergei would die at the end. The only variation on the theme was whether he died with him. Until yesterday, that part of the dance didn't matter.

But now? Now, he had more to live for.

He grabbed the thug's coat and pulled him down. As Sergei struggled, Nikolai kicked him in the torso several times, then threw him across the ground.

As he watched Sergei struggle to his feet, he had the odd sensation that he was being watched. He moved to the side trying to capture a glance of who it was, while not losing sight of Sergei.

In between two birch trees, Patrice stood, motioning him to his forgotten knife. He stole a glance and noticed, through the break in the trees, the frozen lake.

He glanced back at Patrice. She winked and nodded.

Sergei was on his feet. He was breathing hard and seething.

Nikolai bent to pick up the knife.

Sergei came at him at a full run.

Nikolai stalled as the man gathered speed.

Sergei had every intention of barreling into him, holding him down, and killing him.

He wasn't far now. Sergei tucked his head down, ready to make contact. But when he reached his goal, Nikolai stepped to the side.

With nothing to stop him, Sergei flew past him and onto the lake. His legs went every which way.

The sound of the rushing water got louder as he skidded across the lake, toward the falls. Helpless, Sergei rolled to his side to stop his sliding but landed in the rushing water. He was carried away.

Nikolai and Patrice raced along the bank toward the falls. They reached the edge of the cliff and saw Sergei bobbing in the water, headed toward them.

Nikolai quickly laid on the ground and reached out to Sergei. "Grab my hand," he shouted above the rushing water.

The rushing water carried Sergei toward them. He had a helpless look on his face. He raised his arm, reached for Nikolai's, and caught it.

Hanging on tight, Nikolai pulled against the current to haul him from the water.

Sergei glared at him, his mouth in an evil grin.

Nikolai had an uncomfortable feeling and braced himself.

Sergei tugged on his arm.

Nikolai slid closer to the edge.

"He's trying to pull you in." Patrice grabbed him around his waist and held onto him.

Again, Sergei tugged, but the water was turning both men's fingers numb.

Patrice pulled hard. "You can't let him win the game."

Nikolai glanced at her. "No, he's not the game master." He looked at Sergei. "He is just a petty thief and hired assassin." With a quick jerk of his hand, Nikolai was free.

Sergei looked at him in surprise as he was swept over the falls to the rocks forty feet below.

The brooch, the document, Edgemont's game, and the assassinations were all linked. Sergei and Yuri were small players who were expendable. He needed to find the mastermind of this plot. Until he did, Patrice wasn't safe.

They made their way back to the house.

━━━━━◈━━━━━

# CHAPTER EIGHTEEN

P ATRICE SAT COMFORTABLY in the crook of Nikolai's arm in front of the hearth.

"You have surprised me at every turn of this adventure." Something in Nikolai's tone overwhelmed her, made her ache.

She said nothing. Inwardly, she was pleased. Using her mind made her feel alive.

"You're levelheaded and put the pieces together quickly, in a logical way. It's impressive. Many men can't do that." There was admiration in his voice. She hadn't realized how much she wanted his approval. He gave it willingly, without any conditions.

"It comes from years of playing games. You don't panic. You think your way out and use your skills as well as information you pick up along the way."

A loud knock on the front door interrupted them.

They looked at each other.

"It might be Henry." She got up and went to the window. "Oh. What is George Armstrong doing here? Wait here."

Patrice went to let George in.

"George. I didn't expect to see you here." They walked up the stairs to the parlor. Nikolai was gone. She took a seat, but he preferred to stand. He began nervously pacing between the hearth and window.

"You surprised me, and your parents, when we found you

had left to return here. I know I should have contacted you, told you why I was gone. I assure you it was for a family matter. But I returned to tell you—"

A soft cough emanated from the parlor door.

A glancing shadow of surprise washed over George's face before he replaced it with an indifferent expression.

"Mr. Armstrong. Let me introduce you to Grand Duke Nikolai Baranov of the House of Breuce." She turned to him. "Your Grace, George Armstrong."

"Mr. Armstrong?" Nikolai stared at the man and entered the room carrying a bottle of brandy.

"It's much easier on the English to use an English name they can pronounce." He turned to Patrice. "My name is Grigori Petrova. My family has been doing business with the Edgemonts for many years."

"Is your explanation given to excuse you from lying to me for almost a year? I think not."

He sauntered over to one of the wing-backed chairs by the hearth as if he was the lord and master.

"I'm here for a simple business transaction." He glanced at Nikolai, an I-dare-you-to-interfere smile on his face. "I want the same thing His Grace wants. The difference is, I won't take no for an answer. You see, His Grace," he spat out Nikolai's title, "knows what I am capable of."

Nikolai gave him a lazy, bored look and turned to Patrice. "Humor him before I toss him out. He is just like his father, full of bluster when he has someone else around to do his dirty work. Patrice holds the cards." Nikolai turned to George.

"She told you about my gift? I thought it was such a nice touch." George stood and took a glass of brandy. He had the audacity to chuckle. "Her face was precious when she opened the box and saw the deck of cards. You were quite right, you know. It was a jab at your brother. He had the nerve to try to cheat me. I taught him a lesson."

"But not at cards." Nikolai turned his attention from Patrice.

"Everyone knew he cheated at cards." Patrice gave a nervous laugh. "He was tossed out of his club. Father couldn't fix that, although he did try. Cheat you? No one of any worth would sit in a game with him. Did you bait him as you did me?"

"Your brother took something that was mine. I wanted it back." George put his glass down and took Patrice's hands. "I admit, I thought to tease the information from you. But I quickly—"

She snapped her hands out of his. "Please. Don't make more of a fool of yourself than you already are. Or of me."

She stepped toward him, making him back up while she glared at him like an angry schoolteacher reprimanding a student. "You played on my greatest weakness." She stabbed him in his chest with her finger. "And you planned it and took great pride in it." Another stab. "You thought with your overtures I would hand you Edgemont's business." Another stab. "But I, a woman, prevented you from taking it." Another stab. His back was up against the hearth. "I didn't think Mr. Peters was an honest man, but you, you are much worse."

"Do you think your Grand Duke is any better? He wanted—"

"How I deal with His Grace," she snapped at him like an angry dog, her voice low and deadly, "and what he wants is none of your concern. Do. You. Hear. Me. None."

George remained quiet. Nikolai remained vigilant. She remained adamant.

She saw George calculating his next move. She didn't move fast enough.

In a flowing sweeping movement, George grabbed Patrice, spun her about with her arm locked behind her back.

"I want the Royal Brooch. It wasn't with the jewels that were returned to you. Where is it?"

"I have no idea. What makes you think I have it?" She kept her voice even yet patronizing.

"I think you have it because your former solicitor was to meet me here and give it to me. But Sergei and Yuri got out of hand as they did at Philby's office." He looked at Nikolai. "I had no idea *you* were the vagabond in his office. Although it is a boon. You've been an annoyance long enough.

"I was disturbed searching him. When I finally did, all I found were a few coins in his pocket. Someone had to have the brooch and you two were the last ones with him. Where is it?"

"I still have no idea. Perhaps you shouldn't have killed Mr. Peters before he gave it to you. Not very good planning on your part."

George jerked her arm up. Patrice winced but refused to cry out.

"Peters? That wasn't his name. When I met him in St. Petersburg, it was Osip Petrova." Nikolai glared at George.

"Who is Osip Petrova?" Neither man said anything. It was Nikolai's smile that told her all she needed to know. She tried to turn and look at George. "He was your brother. How could you kill your own brother?"

"Don't deceive yourself. You're just like me. How many times did you want to kill your brother?"

"Don't you dare compare me to you. We are not alike. I may not like what Brian did or what he became, but I would never harm him."

"And I thought we made the perfect couple. You won't be surprised that I will not hesitate to kill you and him," he nodded toward Nikolai, "if you don't give me the brooch."

"She has no idea where it is. I do." Nikolai gave him an icy stare.

Patrice searched Nikolai's face. He must have taken the pin from the table, and from the look in his eye he was tempted to throw the pin at George and let him be gone. But they both knew giving him the pin was not going to keep them safe. George wasn't going to leave anyone behind who could tell the tale.

The sound of horses under the portico got her attention.

"I couldn't have planned this better." A large grin spread across George's face. "We'll all go to the door and let our guests in. I'm sure you're eager for a reunion, Your Grace."

NIKOLAI LED THE way to the door. George, with Patrice still in an armlock, followed behind.

Nikolai couldn't count on anything with George. He was a magician of sorts. Every time he thought he had him, he managed to get away. There were several people he could have at his beck and call, even here in England. Any number of them would be dead set against the documents seeing the light of day.

George, still holding Patrice, maneuvered his way close to the door. All Nikolai could do was stand by and watch.

"Sergei?" George called over his shoulder.

Had the man survived the tumble over the falls? The mist from the falls and the curtain of snow made it impossible to see where or if he landed.

"Dah."

George would pit Sergei against him, like a cock fight. If Nikolai won, he'd have to take on George next. Mentally, he was ready. He didn't entertain the thought of losing.

George tightened his hold on Patrice. His mouth to her ear, his eyes never left Nikolai. "You are coming with me. For making me come after you to this bleak little village in the middle of nowhere, you will sign the business over to me willingly or," he paused, "unwillingly. Either way will do."

Patrice kept her eyes on Nikolai. He hoped he gave her strength. They both remained quiet and unmoved. The little repartee was for his benefit. To prove who was the master.

With his free hand behind him, George opened the door wide still focused on Nikolai.

Nikolai blinked and his mouth slowly widened in a smile.

A blanched glaze covered George's face. He turned to see who was at the door.

"Dah, or is it neyt?" Barrington's playful look turned deadly.

Nikolai pulled Patrice out of George's grasp. Then he swung George around and hit him with a right hook. George crumpled to the ground.

"Hold." Barrington stepped between them.

With Patrice at his side, Nikolai was breathing hard, his fists flexing as his rage subsided. He would have pummeled George if Barrington hadn't stepped in front of him.

"Help me bring him upstairs." Barrington motioned to Nikolai.

The fire snapped in the hearth. Patrice stood to the side as Barrington and Nikolai brought George into the parlor and tied him to one of the chairs. When they were done, they sat there as if everyone had a tied-up traitor in their house.

"When I saw you, I thought you were here to tell me about Henry." Patrice looked at Barrington, relieved he was the person at the door.

"The boy was found earlier at Widow Green's. She sent word that the boy was with her. She gave him hot chocolate for his valiant effort in giving her a Valentine's card and he promptly fell asleep. He's back with his family."

"That is a relief. If Henry has been found, what are we waiting for?" Patrice looked from Nikolai to Barrington.

"Not what. Who." Nikolai didn't take his eyes off George.

"He has long been a person who we believed was a traitor." Barrington sounded relieved.

"Traitor to which country, Britain or Russia? One man's allegiance is easily explained as another's treachery." Patrice sat close to Nikolai.

Barrington and Nikolai turned to her, impressed with her observation.

George gloated. "Well put. I knew you were smart."

"You left out France," Nikolai said. "And any country or person that got in his way for power and money. Including Edgemont's money.

The only allegiance George has is to himself."

"You will never prove that." George, though bound to the chair, was smug.

"That was why you needed the Royal Brooch and would do anything to get it."

Nikolai glared at him from across the room.

"There is a document with the names of Napoleon's supporters. People who would rally should he ever come back to power." Barrington leaned forward to get Patrice's attention. "The list is long. It includes Grigori Petrova, George Armstrong."

Patrice turned her attention to George. His smug expression had turned to an icy one.

"What does the gem have to do with the list of conspirators?" She couldn't tie the gem to the document.

Barrington settled back into the chair.

"Members of Napoleon's elite Old Guard were disbanded when he abdicated but have remained close. Many like George serve him, some went with him to Elba." Barrington kept his eyes on George.

"They amassed a list of families sympathetic to Napoleon. People they can rely on should he return to power," Nikolai said. "He suffered a great defeat in Russia. One he is not likely to forget."

"Napoleon has tried to defeat Britain at every turn. With the alliance, we prevail," There was pride in Barrington's voice.

"He was tried, lost, abdicated, and exiled. He will never rise to power again." Patrice was certain.

However, when she glanced at George, a chill went up her spine. His smug expression annoyed her. He knew something that none of them knew. She realized Barrington and Nikolai had the same feeling.

The light was fading outside. There was another knock at the door.

Barrington rose at the same time as Patrice.

"If I may, Lady Edgemont." He went to the door without

waiting for her response. He returned moments later with a tall gentleman flanked by two staff.

Nikolai rose to his feet, clicked his heels, and gave a swift bow.

"Prince Baranov. It is good to see you."

"And you Prince Blucher. I didn't know you were in England."

"The English king was very welcoming. Everywhere I go I am enthusiastically cheered. I must be careful, or it will go to my head." The Prussian officer turned to George. "It will be my pleasure to take you to Prussia. You have made some important people angry. It will give me great satisfaction to deliver you to them."

Blucher signaled to his men. They removed the rope restraints and replaced them with chains.

As they took him out, George hesitated as he passed Patrice. She turned her back. The guards moved him on.

She glanced at Nikolai. His sad expression told her there was no hope for the man.

"He made his decision long ago. He ordered the deaths of many people including Edgemont, my brother-in-law, and my father. He knew the consequences for treason." Nikolai squeezed her hand and released it.

"Lady Edgemont."

Patrice turned toward Prince Blucher, surprised he was aware of who she was.

"I knew your husband. He was a brave and good man." He took her hand in both of his. "I was sorry to hear about his death. I was very fortunate to have known him."

He looked at the doorway. His men returned and nodded.

"I didn't want to say anything with Petrova in the room. There are two rumors. One, Napoleon has been playing the sleeping dragon. Even his subjects on Elba sense it. Two, the documents we're looking for are at the Church at St. Catherine. Before you ask, I do not know who at the church has the document. But that doesn't matter. We haven't got the token to rescue them. Now, if you will excuse me. Barrington, Baranov, Lady Edgemont. I'll see myself out."

He gave a nod and left. Moments later, she heard the door softly close.

"Is Edgemont's name in this document?" Her voice was so low. She was afraid of the answer.

"Not at all." Nikolai moved to the end of his seat and took her hand. "The reason I was here was to obtain confirmation that Edgemont worked with the British, Russian, and Prussian governments. I got that confirmation from Donald Philby, a British agent." He took the paper out of Philby's coat pocket and gave it to her. "Edgemont was not a traitor."

"St. Petersburg," is all Barrington said. "What is the use of knowing where the documents are if we cannot see them."

Nikolai took the Royal Brooch from his pocket and handed it to Barrington.

"How?" was all Barrington could say.

"Today is Tuesday. It's my day for dead bodies." Nikolai and Patrice both burst into laughter.

Barrington stared at both of them. They quieted down.

"When I went to the lodge looking for Henry, I found Nikolai. He was injured. I bandaged him as best I could then we started back here. We found someone had broken the back gate." Patrice tried to be concise.

"We found Peters in the maze pavilion. Dead. He'd been executed. The brooch was in his pocket. I wasn't sure at the time why he had it with him. He was waiting to give it to his brother. At least that is what George told us."

Nikolai waited for Barrington to take it all in.

"I'll see to Peters." Barrington stood with them, deep in thought for several minutes. "Nikolai, you must leave for St. Petersburg at once. You have the token, speak the language, and they know you."

"It's not that easy. I can't simply walk into the church and say,

'Give me the document.'" The frustration in Nikolai's voice was evident.

"But I can." Patrice sat and stared at Barrington and Nikolai's confused expression.

"I received a letter from a priest, expressing his condolences at Edgemont's passing. He is looking forward to me visiting. He feels compelled to bless me. I thought it was strange, but not so now."

Nikolai leaned toward her. "Do you remember the priest's name?"

"I'm sorry. I don't. I accepted it as a compassionate message, one I needed to acknowledge."

"It may be a standard message he sends to families of the recently deceased." Barrington doubted her as well.

"I didn't go to the church or meet any clergy when I was in St. Petersburg. No. There is something more to this. I have the letter with my things at Lady Marianna's."

Barrington got to his feet. "If what you have provides the information we need, then I think we all may be going to St. Petersburg. Once we review the priest's document we can decide. Be prepared to leave for London in the morning. I'll send word to my brother to arrange passage.

"I'll return shortly with a carriage. Lady Edgemont, I'd like to see the letter you received from the church. Besides, Henry has been found. There is no need for you to stay here. Even though George is no longer an issue, we cannot be sure someone else isn't involved. These men are not above using you as a pawn. It would be best if you were my guest at Sommer Chase, where we can be assured you and Jean will be safe. I'll have a guard posted for your safety."

"That won't be necessary." Nikolai got to his feet. "I will guard them."

# CHAPTER NINETEEN

"THANK YOU FOR your hospitality." Patrice was in her room at Ravencroft Manor with Jean. While her maid packed their things, she went through the letters, found the one from the priest, and put it in her reticule. The others she tucked into her portmanteau. "I'll explain everything when I return."

"Gossip is just as bad here as it is in London. What happened that George Armstrong was taken to the dungeon at the castle? You can't leave without telling me."

Patrice had to choose her words carefully. Not an invention, but not the whole story. The fact was, she didn't know it all herself. At least not yet.

"Peters and George were at The Mooring. They thought it would be vacant and didn't expect me to arrive."

"I should never have let you go alone." Anna was horrified.

Patrice stopped her packing and went to her friend and put her arm around her.

"You are truly a good friend. I appreciate that you would do that for me. More than you know.

"They had some of my missing jewels that were stolen while I was in St. Petersburg. Barrington arrived and took care of everything. Because the matter happened while I was out of the country, he is taking me to London to speak to his brother."

Anna seemed almost physically relieved. But quickly asked,

"How did they get your jewels?"

"That is why we are going to London. One of the pieces they had belonged to the Russian royal family. Barrington wants me to speak to Lord Edward." This explanation was creating itself and was almost too easy. "As a member of the House of Lords, Barrington's brother will know what needs to be done. The last thing he wants is an international incident."

"Oh, dear. Do you need someone to go with you? I can be ready."

"Anna, you are a great friend, but no. Jean will be with me."

She glanced at Jean as she closed the last bag and stood it next to the door.

"We must be off. Please let Mrs. Bainbridge and the others know. I will tell you everything when I return."

"You're not leaving for London now, are you?"

Patrice walked with Anna to the bedroom door. Jean had already called a footman to take the bags to the waiting coach.

"I'm staying at Sommer Chase this evening. We leave for London before dawn." Patrice and Anna made their way down the stairs to the main foyer.

"You are a brave woman. Knowing you both are with Barrington calms my concerns. But be wary. The news from the continent has been rife with unrest. I had hoped you would not go back. But do what you must. I'll let the others know."

"You are a dear to let me disrupt your life with my comings and goings."

"Don't let anyone know, but I enjoy it. Now go."

Patrice and Jean hurried out to the waiting carriage. In moments they were on their way.

WHEN PATRICE AND Jean arrived at Sommer Chase, the footman took the luggage and Jean to their room while Patrice was directed to Barrington in the library.

She found him making arrangements for the journey. Nikolai was with Barrington's valet, Kenworth, who was tending his wound.

"Baranov will join us shortly. Kenworth told me you did a wonderful job doctoring the patient. He didn't need any stitches and there was no sign of infection."

"I thought I heard you arrive." Nikolai entered the room.

Her heart skipped a beat. It wasn't a vagabond who stood before her, but the Grand Duke of the House of Breuce. His hair was trimmed, and he was clean shaven. His clothes were the latest fashion. He looked as he did when they first met. It was odd, but she missed his romantically wild hair and his beard.

He stroked his face. "I've had the beard for so long, I miss it." He offered her a seat.

"So do I." She heard his soft chuckle and shook her head. But she was there for more important matters. Patrice sat across from Barrington and took a sheaf of paper from her reticule. "I brought the letter from the priest. It is a short two paragraphs, but odd."

"Why is that?" Barrington gave her his full attention.

"As Lord Edgemont's long-time confessor," she read from the message. She looked at both men.

"Edgemont wasn't Catholic. This priest couldn't be his confessor."

"What is the priest's name?" Nikolai seemed eager to know.

She looked down the page. "Brother Alfredo." She glanced back at him.

"The priest was not his confessor." Nikolai sat back calmly. "Edgemont and Brother Alfredo never met. Brother Alfredo was once part of Napoleon's elite Old Guard. He had access to documents and information that the coalition forces have found useful."

"Why don't you read what Brother Alfredo sent you." Barrington encouraged her on. Both men's attitudes had changed significantly. This message must be more important than she thought.

"Lady Edgemont, please forgive this intrusion. As Lord Edgemont's long-time confessor, I feel compelled to contact you at this time even though we have not been formally introduced. It's difficult to remain silent for a collection of reasons. I am touched by your circumstances, and I have come to offer my sincere sympathy and humble prayers only to you, most-urgently. I was recently made aware of the unbelievable circumstances of your catastrophe.

"I offer you my priestly blessing at my parish house in St. Petersburg to help you heal. Be assured I sympathize with you. May God be with you."

Patrice put the paper on Barrington's desk in front of him to read.

"This asks that I urgently come to St. Petersburg for a blessing, which sounds as if he needs it more than I," she said. "This is nothing."

Nikolai took the brooch from his pocket and placed it on the document.

"Do you think there is a connection between the priest's condolence message and the brooch?" Patrice asked.

Nikolai rose and stood behind Barrington studying the document. He picked up the brooch and examined it.

"There are several key words here." Barrington took a piece of foolscap from the desk. He listed the words.

Urgent. Catastrophe. Church. St. Petersburg.

"There's more to the message than those words." Nikolai moved the priest's note closer. "When I was getting people out of Moscow, we developed an easy system for passing information. Edgemont explained it to me. Only certain words in the message were meaningful. You had to know the key, the magic number. It changed daily."

"There are nine words between catastrophe and church. The one before catastrophe is sincere. No, that's not the number."

Barrington studied the note.

"What would be a significant number for the priest?" Nikolai studied the document.

"Not the priest, a significant number that I would know." Patrice's face lit. "Twelve. I was born and married on the twelfth of April. When we chose the day, I told him he would be in twice as much trouble if he forgot it."

"That was why your dinner in St. Petersburg was important. It was—" Nikolai looked at her his eyes wide in surprise. "April twelfth."

"Yes. April twelfth, our second anniversary. I won't tell you which birthday."

"I'll read the words." She took up the paper.

"I'll write them down." Nikolai took a piece of paper and pencil from Barrington.

"Ready?" She waited for Nikolai's nod and began. "I have collection come urgently catastrophe St. Petersburg."

All three of them stared at the words.

Patrice reread the words. It was a coded message. It was difficult for her to comprehend that Edgemont was involved. But Brother Alfredo was making an urgent appeal.

As Barrington and Nikolai made their plans, she sat and reread the message and realized she knew very little about Edgemont.

"If you will excuse me," she said as she stood. Both men gave her their attention. "It has been a long day."

Nikolai came to her side and walked her to the stairs. "Get a good night's sleep. We have a long journey ahead of us."

She started up the stairs.

"Patrice."

She stopped and turned.

"You are an exceptional woman. Facing George could not have been easy."

She came down the few steps and stood eye to eye with him.

"I had already decided he could not be trusted. But you? I had my doubts at first, but something deep inside told me to trust you."

She kissed his forehead, turned, and went up the stairs.

"I'll see you and Barrington in the morning," she called over her shoulder. She didn't hesitate when she reached the landing. She continued to her room.

⫷⫸

NIKOLAI WAITED UNTIL he heard the soft click of her door closing then he returned to Barrington.

"It's getting late," Barrington was sitting in the parlor. "I have my concerns about bringing Lady Edgemont into this. She's quite clever, but still. We both do not know what we face."

"She'll keep her head about her. I don't think Brother Alfredo will surrender the document to either of us even if we handed him the brooch. There are other words in his message that made that very clear."

Nikolai took the paper and pointed to them. *Only to you.*

"He will only give it to her." Nikolai had his own fears. He was going on instinct and what he observed in one day. They were all he could rely on. He hoped he was right, and that Patrice was up to the challenge.

"You know she will ask you to explain everything. Honoria, Mrs. Bainbridge, assured me Lady Edgemont was more than capable for the task, and keeping her in the dark would be our biggest liability."

Barrington's words made Nikolai look up.

"According to Honoria, if faced with a situation, Lady Edgemont will take action with or without all the facts and that, she said, could cause her to make a dangerous decision."

"She reacted aggressively with George, Sergei, and Yuri. She did not have the vapors. No. The woman is capable and brave. Prepared with the information and including her in our plans will make her a valuable asset."

Barrington sat back in the armchair, deep in thought.

Nikolai picked up the London paper. "There is a great deal of speculation about Napoleon. Not everyone is convinced he will gracefully fade into oblivion in Elba. The information we have access to is urgently needed. This journey is too important to fail. She is a key player in this game. Mrs. Bainbridge is very perceptive. Lady Edgemont deserves to know the who, what, where, and why of things as well as to be included in developing the how."

"There is still the possibility that once she knows it all she won't want to be involved." Barrington looked worried.

"From what you told me of Lady Edgemont when you were growing up, I would think you had a better opinion of her."

"I do." Barrington stared at him. "This *game*, as you refer to it, killed her husband. I don't want it to kill her."

"She will not be alone. Even in Russia, a woman needs an escort. A grand duke should be sufficient."

Barrington nodded. "Especially when the grand duke is you. There is a great deal of information for her to absorb. And she's come to some conclusions for which she wasn't given all the facts."

"Yes. I am aware. We have a ten-day journey ahead of us. It will give us time to give her the information she needs as well as time for her to embrace it."

"I'm glad that's settled. I am to bed. See you in the morning." Barrington gave him the note and the brooch. "I put more than these in your care."

# CHAPTER TWENTY

NIKOLAI PICKED UP the *Sommer Sentinel*, but quickly gave up on it. It had little content. He took Barrington's London paper and made himself comfortable for a long night. He needed time to decide what to tell Patrice in the morning.

He was deep into reading the comments of the situation in France and Belgium when the library door opened.

"You're up early." Patrice entered carefully closing the door not wanting to disturb anyone in the house. "Or haven't you slept?"

"I wanted to read what I could about the situation on the continent." Nikolai lowered the newspaper and glanced at the clock on the mantel. "Two in the morning. Do you usually wake this early?"

"Not at all. I couldn't sleep." Clad in her dressing gown, Patrice swept across the room and sat in the chair facing Nikolai. "I've been turning things over in my mind. I have so many questions."

He put the paper away and gave her his full attention.

"I'll answer whatever I can as candidly as possible."

She gave him a relieved smile.

"When we met in St. Petersburg, I felt guilty that you had to escort me for the evening. I had the impression you wanted to be at the meeting with Edgemont."

"The meeting quickly became unimportant. You were so excited about the ballet and dinner I caught your enthusiasm."

Nikolai knew Edgemont well, but he hadn't met her until that evening. He wasn't surprised that Edgemont refused to disappoint her. After everything that's happened, his father's directive had new meaning.

*"I trust Edgemont but wonder how much Lady Edgemont knows. You're good at this. See what you can find."*

With the way the events developed, Nikolai suspected his father arranged the urgent meeting specifically to find out what Lady Edgemont knew.

Nikolai didn't want to interrogate Edgemont's wife or spend the evening with her. He's suffered through many an evening entertaining wives and daughters for the Tzar and his father. He didn't have much hope for Edgemont's wife.

*"Your Excellency."*

*He turned at the soft lyrical voice and straightened. Lady Edgemont was a vision. Her gown was simple. It was the color of a rich burgundy wine that set off both her red hair and green eyes.*

*"It's a pleasure to meet you." He took her gloved hand and brushed her knuckles with his lips.*

*"It's kind of you to take my husband's place this evening. I was looking forward to the ballet." She removed her hand from his, startling him. Women usually let their hands linger in his.*

"I thought you were kind to put up with me. I could tell by the tilt of your head and stiffness in your shoulders you wanted to be somewhere else."

Nikolai tried to hide that caught-pilfering-a-tart-from-the-kitchen look from his face.

"You're right. But I quickly changed my mind. You weren't affected, offensive, or tactless. Your open and genuine personality captivated me." He put his hand over his heart and gave her an overly passionate look. "You left me no choice but to stop thinking about the meeting."

Patrice covered her mouth to stifle her laughter.

"I had the impression you would rather be at a horse race than at the ballet."

"At the time, a horse race would have been more to my liking." From the expression on her face, she was pleased with his honest answer.

He enjoyed riding, the exhilarating power and mutual respect between the horse and rider. Nikolai glanced at her. "You ride?" The thought rang true in his mind.

"Yes, I do but not in London. I spared Edgemont the embarrassment. I ride only in Sommer-by-the-Sea, where much to his horror, I ride astride." She leaned close to him. "I don't ride sidesaddle."

"You're not afraid?" Her secret fit her character.

"No, not at all. I started riding astride to get away from my brother. You see, riding sidesaddle I couldn't mount the horse by myself. Brian had a fear of horses. Being in the stable and riding was one way to keep him away. When I went to the seminary, I continued to ride astride."

The joy on her face made him want to take her to the steppes outside the city. There, on that vast treeless plain she would enjoy riding. Yes, Lady Edgemont would ride full-out, he was sure of it. And she'd be difficult to catch. When he thought about that, he wondered how Edgemont had caught such a prize.

"I must tell you I have met Olga's match."

He was both surprised and engrossed in what she had to say.

"The mushroom barley soup we had at The Palkin that evening was superb, but I have tasted its match at The Rostov Tearoom in Sommer-by-the-Sea."

"Please, don't mention that to Olga. She'd take you off her list."

Patrice laughed.

"There are other parts of dinner I remember. *Moy lev.*"

"My lion." He squinted his eyes and looked at her. "You said those words to me."

"In the lodge," she nodded, "when you were restless. I can't explain why, but the words came to mind, and I said it. I was surprised that it worked. You looked at me clearly, closed your eyes, and went to sleep."

"*Lishichka.*"

"Little fox." She ran her fingers through her hair. "For my red hair. But it was the vodka ritual I enjoyed the most."

He went over to the sideboard and poured them each a glass of vodka.

"Barrington is a barbarian. He doesn't usually have vodka. However, I came bearing gifts." He handed her a glass.

"I honor the Spirit." She brought the glass to her nose and took a whiff, then raised it high.

Nikolai did the same.

"Na zdrovie za druchbu, to a successful adventure," she said.

"Na zdrovie za druchbu, to a successful adventure," he repeated.

He nodded his admiration and drank his vodka.

She drank from her glass.

"We mustn't forget zakuska, the snack." He handed her a scone from the tray on the sideboard.

"I wanted to remember that night of my visit to Russia. The rest was…" She looked at him, unable to hide the sorrow in her eyes. "Difficult. The following day was a blur. People were in and out of the villa. I didn't see Edgemont until we reached the docks to meet Ambassador Cathcart. The last image I have of Edgemont is of him on the dock as the boat pulled away. He followed the ship until he came to the end of the pier. He stood there until we sailed around the bend."

He could see her chest heaving. He wanted to take her into his arms and console her.

"If you'll forgive me. I'm more tired than I thought." She walked to the door. "I'll see you in the morning." She hesitated and glanced over her shoulder. "I did enjoy dinner that evening."

And she was gone.

⚜

# CHAPTER TWENTY-ONE

PATRICE PUT ON her gloves on her way out of the house. Jean was behind her with a basket that Barrington's housekeeper, Mrs. Tripp, gave them for the journey. Nikolai, Barrington, and Mr. Kenworth finished making certain the coach was loaded and ready for the four-day ride to London. Nikolai handed the ladies up to their seats.

"Ladies," Barrington started. "I must apologize before we begin. The journey in good weather is three days. While the snow has stopped, the weather may not be in our favor. If we do not make good time as planned we will travel at night. It will be uncomfortable for all of us, but it is imperative that we reach London as quickly as possible."

Once they left Sommer-by-the-Sea, they found the road to York was in good condition. They stopped every three hours for thirty minutes to change teams. It was nine in the evening when the coach pulled into a moderately sized farm. The farmer greeted Barrington like an old friend.

"Let me introduce you to my companions." Barrington looked worn, but even tired and under pressure, he managed to remain in good spirits. "This is Lady Edgemont, Mrs. Jean Murray, Nikolai Baranov, and you know Kenworth." Barrington turned to the farmer who stood with two boys. "Everyone, this is First Sergeant Todd Fuller, retired."

"Come inside. Dinner is waiting. My boys will take care of the team." Mr. Fuller scooted the boys out to the waiting team.

The house was cozy and warm. Fuller and his wife, Karen welcomed them in as if they were family. While Barrington, Nikolai, and Fuller traded military stories, she and Karen listened. There was no way they could get a word in if they wanted to.

For a moment she dwelled on her own issue. Nikolai's version of the man she married aligned with the man she grew up with, but she didn't understand why he chose to deceive her. He knew very well what she was capable of.

"You're not enjoying these stories," Nikolai presented it more as a question than a statement.

"It's not that. I've been thinking about our task. I have an observation. I know Barrington is eager to reach London. He seems to get more anxious the closer we get to the city."

"For months, the Tzar has been trying to identify those who support Napoleon. They are not all Frenchmen. Some are Russian. He is diligent about preventing another invasion. So am I.

"A list of Napoleon's supporters was drafted. The originator would not deal with my father, the Tzar, or the coalition. It was to go to Edgemont to give it to his brother, Lord Edward. The originator demanded something of great value in exchange. The brooch was offered, the deal made. The originator gave the list to someone he trusted to make the exchange."

"Brother Alfredo."

"Yes. Now we know it is Brother Alfredo who has the list. In St. Petersburg, Edgemont obtained the brooch. He was ready to execute the exchange when the brooch was stolen. He was the only one who knew where the list was held. The gamer that he was, he told no one.

"The evening I escorted you to the ballet and dinner, my father asked if perhaps you had any information about the list."

"Me?"

"My father said you were a very clever woman. But I already

knew you didn't have the information. Edgemont would not jeopardize you. After the theft of the brooch and your husband's death, no one had any idea where the list was or how they would claim it. Until now."

"That is why Brother Alfredo will only give it to me." She stopped and looked at him. "I represent Edgemont."

Nikolai said nothing.

⋙⋘

BARRINGTON'S EAGERNESS TO get to London had him pushing them on. They traveled ten hours the second day and nine hours the third.

They crossed the River Lee on the outskirts of London in the late afternoon. They were less than seven miles from their destination. The forty-five-minute ride took them a tortuous two and a half hours. They arrived at Barrington Hall after dinner.

Kenworth, who had been sitting next to the coachman, had the luggage out of the carriage and into the foyer before Lord Edward greeted them.

"You must have put wings on those horses' hooves," Lord Edward greeted his brother, holding him close.

"I don't think you know Baranov. Lord Edward—"

"No need for formality tonight." Lord Edward smiled at Nikolai. "I'm pleased to meet you. I hear you've been keeping Reese busy."

"I try my best." Nikolai immediately liked Barrington's brother.

"Lady Edgemont, you remember my older brother, the one who would not let you skate on the ice even though the lake was owned by your family."

"Please do excuse him, Lady Edgemont. He has no sense of what to do around the opposite gender when you're trying to make an impression. He could use a lesson or two." Lord Edward offered her his arm. "Please do me the honor."

Patrice gave him a dazzling smile and as they walked up to the door, she glanced over her shoulder at Nikolai and Barrington, who stood there dumbfounded.

They gathered in the parlor. After the tumult and everyone settled down, Reese Barrington addressed them.

"It was a hard drive, but that will be nothing compared to the six days from here to St. Petersburg."

"He is correct. All the arrangements have been made. I suggest you all get a good night's sleep. You leave tomorrow on the early morning tide. You need to be on the ship by three in the morning."

They said their good nights. Nikolai and Patrice started up to their rooms.

"You've been very quiet most of this afternoon. Are you having second thoughts?"

"No. Not at all."

"You'd tell me if you were. You don't have to do anything you don't want to do."

"I am fine with speaking to Brother Alfredo." She stared at him. Starting this adventure she wanted to know everything, every nuance. "I've been thinking about Sergei and Yuri."

Nikolai took her to the window seat not far from their rooms.

"Who were they and what part did they play in all this?"

"It's a fair question. Both were members of the family and worked in the family business. My father kept a close watch on what Sergei and Yuri did and how they did it. Two years ago, something changed. There was unrest within those family members working with my father. The closer my father got to the Tzar's inner circle, the more difficulties he had with his business. It's not uncommon for members of the board to vie for control. And given father's interests with the Tzar, the power dynamic slowly shifted to someone else.

"After my father died, I went through the company records and clearly saw the pattern. Through misleading financial reports and activities, significant people were convinced he no longer could control the company, so they moved their support to another."

"That's what started to happen with Edgemont's company."

"I'm not surprised. The same person was involved in both."

"Peters?"

"George, as you know him."

She was quiet. How easily she could have been duped.

"Neither George nor Peters counted on you being able to stop them. Like my father, Edgemont was aware of Peters' allegiance. Both were careful and used their knowledge wisely. Or at least my father thought he had."

"You're right. Mr. Peters didn't expect me to understand the business reports. I was so angry with his condescending attitude when I asked to see the accounts and financial records. He was so smug when he gave me the ledgers, daring me to look inside. I left an hour later and came back with Mr. Lacey who removed Peters from Edgemont's office.

"I understand George and Peters wanted both my father's and Edgemont's businesses, but why?"

Nikolai drew in a deep breath. It was a question he hoped he wouldn't have to answer, for her protection. He took her hands in his and looked into her eyes. She trusted him and deserved an answer.

"I mentioned that I worked for the Tzar and gave you the evidence that Edgemont worked for the King."

"I still find Edgemont's work for the King difficult to believe." She released his hands and rose.

She moved toward her room. She stopped when she reached the door, her hand on the latch.

"Their business ventures concealed the true nature of their work. George didn't care about the financial gains." Patrice glanced at him. "He was after the political gains, access to the Tzar and the King."

He neither denied nor confirmed anything. He didn't have to.

Her cool reaction confirmed he was correct about her and her ability with this assignment.

"It makes me more determined to see this through. Thank you. I'll see you in the morning." She stepped into her room and quietly closed the door behind her.

He let out a breath. There was more for her to know. Let her digest this. He'd be ready when she asked.

THEY SAILED OUT of London on the HMS Redoubtable. The cold temperature and steady wind on the North Sea had them staying in the captain's lounge or their cabin most of the voyage. The rough seas tossed the ship, making it difficult to stay put, let alone walk. The short days with limited sunlight were melancholic and gloomy. When they reached the Baltic Sea, it wasn't much better. The weather was far too cold to be enjoyable.

The ship docked at St. Petersburg mid-morning as planned, with everyone eager to set foot on land. A troika waited for them.

Patrice had ridden in horse-drawn sleighs. This one was larger and more decorative, but much the same. Her attention was drawn to the magnificent horses that were harnessed three-abreast.

The grey Russian stallion was taller than the standard breeds she knew. Standing next to the lead horse, she had an urge to mount up and ride, feel its speed.

"You are a beauty." She stroked the long-arched neck. The horse turned and looked at her. "You're welcome."

In answer, the horse shook its head and nickered.

"He likes you." Nikolai stood next to her patting the horse's neck. "He doesn't always like to be stroked, unless there is an apple to be had."

He handed her up to the troika and tucked a fur blanket around her.

"It's a short ride, but in this weather and with their speed, it can be cold."

The others on board, they took off at a fast canter and flew across the snow. The only time she had gone this fast was when she slid down the ramp in the icehouse.

In much too short a time than she would have liked, the sleigh came to a stop in front of a large villa. It looked similar to Lord Percy's summer house, a three story, quadrangular stone building with turrets, around a central, open courtyard.

She was shown to her room and after freshening, Patrice made her way to the family parlor. It was a comfortable room, with enough room for a small grand party. She grasped the back of the nearest piece of steady furniture.

Seating areas were casual and plush. The wool carpets covered the floor. A large chandelier in the center of the room holding close to twenty-five candles lit the room. The walls were a dove grey with gold and peach accents. The curtains at the great windows matched the walls. In front of the fireplace was a table set for two.

Nikolai stood as she entered the room. He'd been sitting at the writing desk on the other side of the room, reviewing documents.

"Please, there is no need to be so formal. You seem to have gotten your land legs back. Mine," she navigated a few more steps, "are taking their time."

"Don't despair. Barrington is having trouble standing without falling over. He asked to be excused this evening. I'm glad you want to be less formal. I took the liberty of having a light supper served here."

"You have a lovely grand dining room. I would have to get up each time I wanted to talk to you, the table seats fifty, on each side."

He chuckled, a musical sound, or was she just tired? "My mother used to demand we eat there even when it was the four of us. While the room has its uses and it is beautiful, I prefer something less… ornate."

He helped her to her chair. She took the linen, opened it, and placed it on her lap.

"I've sent word to Brother Alfredo that you and I wish to see him. He has agreed to an audience tomorrow, late morning."

The footman came in with a tureen and served them.

Patrice looked at the bowl, then at Nikolai.

"It's red."

He said nothing.

"I expected mushroom barley soup." She didn't hide the disappointment in her voice.

He almost laughed at how crestfallen she appeared.

"Olga isn't in the kitchen. She lives with my sister. This is another peasant soup, borscht. It's made with meat, beets, and other sauteed vegetables. It's very good, especially when it's eaten with a fermented cream."

He spooned a dollop of cream from the serving dish into his bowl.

Patrice followed suit, then tentatively tasted it.

"It has a sweet and savory taste." She paused. "It's delicious."

"I'm relieved. I thought I would have to send for Olga, and she is a very long distance away."

She paused for a moment.

"It was clear from what you've told me Mr. Peters was not aligned with George. How was he involved in the current situation?" Patrice asked.

Nikolai paused, his spoon halfway to his mouth.

She could see him weighing what to tell her. What would make him hesitate? What could be so terrible? Or did he think she would swoon? Hadn't he realized she was made of stronger stuff? Had she touched on a sore subject? Was he involved? She took another spoonful of soup and tried to act as if she was eager for his answer.

He put the spoon down and wiped his lips with the linen.

She took another spoonful as if she wasn't waiting on tenterhooks, as if the sweet soup hadn't turned to vinegar in her mouth.

"Peters." Nikolai took a deep breath. She glanced at him. "Peters was aligned with your brother, Brian."

The spoon dropped from her hand. "No. That can't be true. What could Brian have to do with this?"

"In a way, everything. Edgemont told me Brian demanded he be made a partner in his business. Edgemont said no. Your brother became angry and made threats."

"I'm not surprised. He never wanted to work for his money just spend everyone else's. He came to me a week after Edgemont's funeral with the same demand. He became almost uncontrollable when I refused. Edgemont did not include Brian in any of his dealings. How does this all fall to him?"

"Brian was trying to get into Edgemont's business. He needed to know what was happening, so he became close friends with Peters. It didn't take him long before he realized Peters was stealing from Edgemont. Every deal that was completed, Peters took money before reporting it to Edgemont."

"And once Brian had that information, he blackmailed Mr. Peters."

Nikolai nodded. "It wasn't a great deal of money. It was enough that Peters became Brian's primary source of income."

"Yes, when I went over the company accounts I found financial improprieties. That's when I hired Mr. Lacey. We gave Mr. Peters his notice. He never revealed the funds went to Brian. Mr. Lacey and I assumed he took the money for himself."

"Your trip to St. Petersburg was not a quiet event. The British ambassador as well as the Prime Minister were aware you and Edgemont were going. It created a perfect opportunity for your brother."

"How? He wasn't with us." Patrice's feet wiggled nervously under the table. "He was with Edgemont before dinner the night before our voyage. I assumed it was to badger him for money. Before he left he came to my room. I remember him looking through my jewel case as we spoke."

"Were you close?" Nikolai's question was casual, but she had the impression he was interrogating her.

"Dear Lord, no. Not at all." She tossed her serviette onto the table. "Nothing was ever enough for him. He wanted whatever I had. 'His birthright,' he'd tell me." She looked away from him, trying to regain some control before she burst into flames. "When he left, I had Jean count the pieces to make sure they were all there."

*A deep breath. That's it. Now another.* Slowly, her thundering heart settled back to normal.

"When he found out that Peters was going with you and Edgemont, he increased his price. When Peters couldn't pay, Brian suggested he take your jewels, make it look like a theft. While I cannot be certain, I am left to assume that after a few months, when the theft was forgotten, he would have Peters sell them."

"No, that couldn't be. Mr. Peters was at the meeting with Edgemont," she said.

"As was George." Nikolai was narrowing down the candidates.

"Sergei and Yuri? Do you think," her face blanched at the very idea, "they came into my room?"

Nikolai let out a deep breath. "Yes. My father sent them to guard the villa. But they are petty thieves. They do not think on their own. You saw what happens when they do. No. Someone told them what to do and how to do it."

"They were astute enough to get into my room and take my jewels without waking me."

"But not much else. They emptied the jewel case and left. By the time they arrived at the meeting place, Peters was there, took the cache, paid Sergei and Yuri, and hurried away. Peters didn't want to be seen with them. It wasn't until he looked at the gems that he found the brooch."

"Peters traveled with us back to London. You're saying he had the jewels and the brooch with him the entire time?" She paused. "If you're saying he or his brother is so clever, then I'm not sure Peters had any plans of being noble. The brooch was worth much more than my jewels. Without access to Edgemont's money, he did have a way to get money from me. But he didn't act on it."

Nikolai moved forward in his seat, his hands resting on the table.

"How?" Nikolai's soothing voice probed farther.

"By going to the Tzar or the King and telling them Edgemont, or I for that matter, planned the theft. His way of revenge. He may have been more ruthless than George or Grigori, whatever he calls himself."

Nikolai stared at her, a gleam of admiration in his eye. He leaned even closer.

"If you are correct, if it was Peters – and if his plan worked – he would be a wealthy man."

"That is on the surface, but what you, Barrington, and Edgemont were about had much greater consequences."

"You, Lady Edgemont, have a devious mind and are quite correct." Nikolai took a deep breath and eased his shoulders. "He could have caused the collapse of two intelligent agencies and gotten access to the information that would have started another war.

"It has to be George. He is the only one alive and in the Sommer-by-the-Sea dungeon. Anyone else involved is dead. We ran through the gauntlet and survived. All we have to do is get our prize, present the brooch to Brother Alfredo tomorrow in exchange for the document."

"If it is that easy, why the somber face?" Patrice asked.

"I don't have an easy feeling. I suppose I never do until an assignment is complete. It may be my ancestors that I don't want to hex things. I'm sure everything will be satisfactory."

"I will do my best to represent Edgemont when I meet Brother Alfredo."

"No." Nikolai stared at her with a grave expression, shaded with trust and pride. "Not Edgemont. You represent England."

# CHAPTER TWENTY-TWO

IT WAS LATE morning when they arrived at the parish house. Neither Nikolai nor Patrice had spoken since they left the villa. He glanced at her proud profile. He and Barrington had done their best to prepare her for this exchange. She knew as much as they did. All three of them were aware it would not be simple. *None of these ever are.* No. This game may be new to Patrice, but she was well aware of the dangers.

They got out of the troika, made their way through the garden to the door. Patrice nodded to Nikolai and gave him a brave smile, one that said she trusted him, one that said she was prepared, one that said she was ready.

Nikolai raised his hand to knock but stopped. The door stood ajar.

"Stay close." Nikolai took her hand and with his other, pushed the door open.

They stood still and silent. Nikolai searched the area and mapped out an escape route and identified where there could be danger and what he could use to his advantage.

The foyer was a modest size with chestnut paneling. The stairs in front of them reached to the upper floors. To the left was a closed door, a parlor, he suspected. To the right of the stairs, a long hall to the back of the house and to the right of the hall, another door that was half-open. The smell of oak and pine drifted out from that room. They were not alone.

An uneasiness crept into Patrice's expression. She moved toward the room. He pulled her back. Before he could say anything, her finger was against his lips, her mouth against his ear.

"Change in plans. Divide and conquer. I'll go in and talk. You come to my aid if needed."

He didn't have a choice. Nikolai gave her a brisk nod.

"You'll never be out of my sight."

She was reading too much Napoleon. This was his tactic. He let out a deep breath. She was right. Every bone in his body told him to be at her side, not behind her. The same bones screamed this was not going to go well.

Patrice stepped inside and he remained a few steps behind. The room was comfortably warm. The high-back chair faced the hearth.

"Hello. Brother Alfredo?" Patrice stopped a few steps behind the chair and waited.

Slowly the priest rose from the chair and faced her. He wore his black mantle with his hood on. It kept the priest's face in the deep shadows.

"Forgive me." His voice was fragile and thin. "The cold weather has taken its toll. While my brothers see to their responsibilities, I remain here. Please, you and your friend be seated." He shuffled around his chair and gestured toward the sofa that was close by.

Nikolai went to her side. They both preferred to stand.

"SOMETHING IS NOT right. Where is his rosary?" Her voice was soft. Only for Nikolai's ears. She took her seat. The holy beads were part of the Black Friar's habit. He would never be without it.

She sensed more than saw Nikolai's concern. He was on high alert.

"Where is Brother Alfredo?" Patrice's voice was exasperated, her stare deadly.

"Patrice?" The man threw back his hood revealing his badly scarred face. "You never did play games as you should. You have to win at everything. You always preferred Edgemont's games to mine."

Patrice had no reaction. Her stare didn't waver.

"Your Grace." Patrice turned to Nikolai. "Let me introduce you to Brian Montgomery. It appears my brother is not dead after all."

"No relief that your little brother is alive and well?" Brian tried to smile, but the scars turned his face into a grimace.

"I was relieved when I received news of your passing. I didn't miss the jealous, selfish, self-absorbed boy. You haven't changed." What was Brian up to and how was he involved in all this? "Is this one of *your* little games?" Her voice dripped with a scornful tone.

"You thought you had made such a good arrangement with Edgemont. He would take care of the family."

"Not at all." Patrice waved off his comment and walked across the room. "I had no care for the family. You made it clear that you would inherit it all and I nothing. The family was to be your responsibility."

Not bothering to face him fully, she glanced over her shoulder at him. "You clearly told Edgemont at our wedding how happy you were that he was taking me off your hands. Now that an allowance wasn't necessary, it would be yours. He told me how gracious you were when you were told the funds were from Grandmama and she had put them in trust for me and were not yours at all."

Brian seethed with anger, and it was building to an explosion. Yes, she was goading him, but it was the only way she could get him to speak without thinking.

"He was impressed when he found that I had managed the

accounts and how they had grown. Well, that was another time."

She noticed the wild look in Brian's eyes. Nikolai must have as well. He stepped closer to her.

"It doesn't matter now. Edgemont is gone and unlike you, he is very dead." She turned back to the window and looked at the snow-covered garden.

"You haven't asked me how I survived."

"I assume something went wrong with your hoax. Your accomplice missed his mark. Something you and," she turned and faced him fully, "Peters planned."

Brian's smug expression melted, replaced with rage.

"It's drastic action, playing dead," Patrice said, the bitterness spilling over in her voice. "But it is one way of avoiding paying your debts. Your death did come with other benefits. I never had to deal with you again. That is, until now. So, what brought you back among the living. Or is it the dead won't have you either?"

"You can't fool me." Brian stepped toward his sister. "Once your jewels were stolen you told everyone the brooch was taken as well when you had it all along." He took another step closer. Nikolai moved between the brother and sister. "The brooch wasn't with the jewels."

"I didn't have it. Peters did. He gave it to me last week."

"Don't lie to me. He was dead last week," he ranted, and raised his hand.

Nikolai grabbed Brian's arm and twisted it behind his back. "Raise your hand to your sister and you will wish you stayed dead." He pushed Brian so hard, he stumbled and fell into the chair.

Nikolai stalked over to the chair. He stood over him, his hands on the arms of the chair locking Brian in place.

"You thought to steal your sister's jewels for your own gains. You had no idea that the brooch was among them. But Peters did. He knew its significance and told his brother."

Nikolai bent closer to Brian.

Patrice watched fear play across her brother's face. God's

pointer finger, she had no compassion for him. Her handsome, sweet brother had been lost to her years ago with the excesses their mother gave him.

"I waited, as Peters and I planned. Months I suffered, waited, and for what?" Brian strained in the chair but was more afraid of Nikolai than getting free. "Peters returned the jewels. But not the brooch. He took it. It wasn't his," his voice raised. "It is mine," a crazed tone to his voice.

"It. Is. Mine." Nikolai's clipped words stopped Brian and surprised Patrice.

"No," Brian insisted. He looked from Nikolai to Patrice. "Armstrong told me. He said it was mine. All I had to do was get it from you and give it to Brother Alfredo. He would give me the treasure. When I didn't have the brooch, I came to Brother Alfredo, but he would not tell me anything. But I waited and planned. You think you're so clever." He took the sheath of paper from inside his robe. "I took the treasure from him. Here it is."

Nikolai stood back. Patrice went to grab the paper, but Brian kept it out of her reach.

"This is what you want? Peters fooled you, too." He shook it in front of them. "It's nothing. Letters that spell nothing. Nothing in English. Nothing in Russian. Nothing in any language."

Patrice glanced at Nikolai. He wasn't surprised or concerned.

"Look at it. A jumble of nothing." He handed his sister the paper.

"Brother Alfredo wouldn't help you, even with his vast knowledge of languages." Nikolai was calm and matter-of-fact. "You have no idea what it says or why anyone would want it. And those who do are either dead or in chains."

"You want it, or you wouldn't be here."

"I will not give you the brooch, Brian." Nikolai's voice had a finality to it that couldn't be denied.

Brian pushed Nikolai away. He grabbed the paper out of Patrice's hand, crumpled it, then tossed it away.

Patrice tried to catch the ball, but Brian knocked it out of her hands toward the fire. They both watched as it hit the inside of the hearth and rolled and smoldered in the hot ash.

Moving quickly, she paid no attention to the scuffle that ensued between Nikolai and Brian. Saving the treasured list was her only thought. Without thinking of the consequences, she reached into the hearth to grab the small ball, but the heat made her pull her hand out.

Nikolai was thrown against the table next to the hearth, books tossed every which way. He righted himself and sprung back into the melee.

Desperate, she grabbed the bottom of her skirt to protect her hand and plucked out the smoldering ball and worked at smothering the singed paper at the same time.

The list wasn't out of danger. She dropped her skirt and took the ball to the window seat as far away from Nikolai and Brian as possible. There, she carefully opened the paper and placed it against the cold window to make sure it wouldn't burst into flames.

She stared at the paper. Brian was correct. It was columns of random letters, like one of Edgemont's games.

A hand reached past her and grabbed the paper. She turned to see Brian running out the door and Nikolai not far behind.

Patrice hurried after them. Her brother was heading for the garden.

Ahead was the garden gate. She had to reach Brian before he got to the troika. Patrice rushed through the gate and came to an abrupt stop. Nikolai stood on the carriage, searching the area.

They glanced at each other. Brian was nowhere to be found.

# CHAPTER TWENTY-THREE

THE HORSES SNORTED loudly and nickered. The lead horse began to dance restlessly in place, his head high, his ears pointed toward the gate, the whites of his eyes showing.

Afraid he'd bolt, she stood next to the beast, speaking softly and trying to soothe him.

The team was calm when she and Nikolai arrived. The only way to calm them was to remove what made them anxious. Patrice followed their stare to the bushes at the side of the gate.

The clang of the church bells made her jump and unsettled the already restless horses.

Patrice grabbed the lead horse's bridle and lowered his head, trying to keep the animal from rearing while she spoke softly to calm him.

Nikolai wrestled with the reins working to quiet the team.

"Patrice!" Brian screamed, as he burst from the bushes.

She swung around toward her brother, struggling to keep her grip on the bridle. The look on Brian's face as he ran toward her, his arms flailing, was a combination of determination and fear. Patrice froze in place.

He was the little boy running toward her, the boy she once cuddled and protected.

Nikolai struggled with the reins to keep the team under control, but the horses, already on edge, were now fully frightened.

Brian, his black habit flying, ran toward Patrice. The horse broke loose from her grip.

Nikolai jumped off the sleigh and reached for the bridle, but the horse threw its head high. The bridle was out of Nikolai's reach.

Brian pulled Patrice away from the horses. The animal reared, screeching, its hooves high in the air. Brian, his arms raised, screamed as he looked at the horse's clawing hooves overhead. The animal struck him as it came down.

Then Brian lay in the mud and snow, bloody and dead.

Before Patrice could reach for her brother, Nikolai pulled her away and held her head to his chest.

A flurry of friars fled the garden and calmed the animals enough to remove Brian.

"Nikolai, take her into the parish house."

"It all happened so quickly." Patrice was shaking in his arms as they walked into the house. She looked up at him. "He pulled me away."

Nikolai sat with her in the parlor which was still in shambles after the scuffle with Brian.

"I've put a splash of spirits into your tea, for medicinal reasons." A friar with a benevolent smile handed her the cup.

She sipped the brew staring at the floor.

"Brother Alfredo, this is Lady Edgemont, Lord Edgemont's widow."

Brother Alfredo's smile slipped into a somber expression.

"I came as soon as I heard the disturbance. I don't know what got into Brian. He's never been violent. Do you know him?"

"Yes, I do." She raised her head and looked at the friar and let out a deep breath. "He's Brian Montgomery, my brother. I didn't know he was here. My family was told he was dead."

"Your Grace, perhaps you should take Lady Edgemont—"

"Thank you for your concern, but no," she interrupted. "I will have time to deal with Brian. I've come a long way because I believe you sent this to me. It seems you also enjoy games." She took the letter she received out of her pocket and handed it to the priest.

Brother Alfredo read it. He gave her an apologetic look. Gone was the pleasant smile. It was replaced with serious determination. "Come with me." He led them across the garden into the church office.

"Lady Edgemont, you have solved one part of the puzzle. Now in order to complete it, you must give me the key."

Patrice took the brooch from inside her pelisse and handed it to the friar. He examined it closely.

"Beautiful. It is the true Royal Brooch."

Brother Alfredo unlocked a small door in the wall and placed the brooch inside. Once he locked it away, he reached for the 1812 church registry and removed a document tucked between two pages. He handed them to Patrice.

She and Nikolai examined a long list of names and locations.

"I don't understand." Patrice looked at both men. She put the list into her reticule, took out the singed paper, and handed it to Brother Alfredo. "This isn't the document you wanted to give me?"

The priest glanced at it and smiled.

"No. This is Brian's document."

"Brian's? I don't understand." She looked from the priest to Nikolai.

"Your brother arrived here nine months ago."

"In May?" Patrice glanced at Nikolai. "That's when he was killed. At least, it's when we were *told* he was killed."

"Yes, May is when he came here. He's been doing odd jobs for us. His accident left him," the friar searched for a word, "not well. We did what we could for him. He was pleasant and helpful. He spent a good deal of time helping the brothers in the garden.

"But he kept getting very bad headaches followed by bouts of disorientation. The more he had headaches, the less he was lucid. We also found he enjoyed puzzles and that seemed to keep his mind active, ward off the headaches. He wrote notes to us in code and challenged us to solve them."

"Code?"

"Yes, he said he used to write them with a friend when he was a boy. That's what this is. I'll read it to you." Brother Alfredo held the document up to the mirror. After a few minutes, he turned back to her. "It's the beginning of Psalm 109. *For wicked and deceitful mouths are opened against me.* And something strange. *God's pinkie.*"

"His friend." Patrice shook her head. "Edgemont. The two were close when we were younger. As we grew up, our relationships changed. Brian never really understood that."

"You're the person who took his friend from him." The friar put the registry away. "I suspect it was difficult for him."

Patrice stared at the friar. Had that been the issue with Brian all these years? A rivalry only he saw. She closed her eyes. *You have to win at everything.*

"You may be correct. After Edgemont and I married, he still wanted all of Edgemont's attention. He'd make up games to please him and got upset when Edgemont gave him a puzzle he couldn't solve but I could."

"You should know that he was happy here. Respected. He and his games will be missed."

PATRICE AND NIKOLAI returned to the villa to wait for Barrington in the family parlor. The room was large with several seating areas, wool carpets covering the floor, and long flowing red drapes at the tall windows. The white walls with their gold leaf stucco frames were filled with family portraits. The central point of the room was the large hearth and the family portrait above it. It was a proud family in state dress.

"God's toes," she blurted out. Patrice turned toward Nikolai. "It's Tanya, Tatiana Chernokov. The tearoom."

"Yes, Anya. She is my sister." He said nothing else.

"How did I not see that? Tanya never said a word." She muttered. She took a closer look. The resemblance between brother and sister was uncanny.

"I asked Tanya not to say anything to you. Barrington and I brought Tanya and Olga to Sommer-by-the-Sea when my father and Leonid were murdered."

"That is why Tanya's soup reminds me of St. Petersburg. I'm glad the truth is out. About everything."

Nikolai stared at her. There was one more truth she had to know. Perhaps the best time to tell her was on the trip back to England when there were distractions.

"Here you are." Barrington barreled into the room. "I was afraid you'd still be with Brother Alfredo. News reached the palace today. Napoleon escaped from Elba Island. Our mission is more important than ever. Were you successful?"

Patrice took the papers out of her reticule and handed them to Barrington.

"You retrieved this at the perfect moment." Barrington scanned through the list. "Some of these names will surprise many people. The Tzar as well as the coalition leaders agree. We must get this to my brother as soon as possible. It will take the English Navy to bring Napoleon to justice now. If we fail, Napoleon will never be stopped."

Barrington took the papers and placed them in a folio he brought with him.

"I'm relieved everything went well with Brother Alfredo."

Patrice looked at Nikolai.

"What happened?"

"My brother was alive," Patrice said, as matter-of-fact as she could.

It was Barrington's turn to look uneasy.

"Brian survived his injury. He was at the church when we arrived. Armstrong manipulated him to believe... It doesn't matter what Brian believed. Armstrong wanted to bring about the downfall of the Montgomery family one member at a time.

His financial manipulation of my father's business and Edgemont's, through his brother, was cut short. His attempt to get to the funds through me didn't work either. That left only Brian. He played on his weaknesses. The staged incident at the gambling den was very successful. He shot Brian in the head badly enough to seriously injure him and make him into his puppet.

"He was terrified of horses but ran to protect me when I was in danger. In his final moments, he was the brother I grew up loving."

"You don't have to continue." Barrington glanced at Nikolai. "If you need some time, Baranov and I can continue alone."

Patrice put on a smile. "Not at all. We are in this together and I will see it through."

"The ambassador will be leaving for England on the evening tide. We will be with him."

"You and Lady Edgemont, but not me."

Patrice tried hard not to react, but it was as if something snapped inside her. A glance at Nikolai and she knew he wanted to go with them.

"No." Barrington didn't look happy. "The Tzar requested you see him in the morning. I told him you would be an asset in London, but he wouldn't hear of it."

"I'm not surprised. My uncle prefers the family around him in a crisis."

Barrington glanced at Nikolai and Patrice and let out a slow breath.

"Ambassador Cathcart is expecting us in two hours. We're sailing directly to Sommer-by-the-Sea. I will rouse my men then Cathcart will bring us to London. I have preparations to make before the tide. If you'll excuse me." Barrington stood and looked at them. She thought he would say something, but instead left the room.

"I thought we'd have more time together." Patrice fidgeted with her fingers and looked off at nothing in particular. Anything so he wouldn't see her disappointment or the tears that threatened. "After this adventure, Sommer-by-the-Sea will seem very dull."

"I cannot imagine life with you ever being dull." For a moment she wished his voice wasn't so soft and mellow.

"You hardly know me," she snipped at him. God's thumb, what was she going to do without him?

"Know you? I knew you long before we met."

Patrice blinked trying to make sense of his comment.

"There are certain truths that you have been led to believe that are false." He took her hands. "Two years ago, Lord Edward made a request to the Tzar. He asked that I work with Edgemont. It was not very long after your wedding."

"That's when he began to travel."

"Yes. We were together through France and Europe, as businessmen. Our days were busy, and our nights were just as long."

"I thought he was entertaining clients. That's what he told me." She turned away from Nikolai. "I didn't even know the true nature of his business. I shouldn't be surprised. Married life was not important to him."

"That's not true."

"There is no need for you to defend him. I came to grips with the truth a long time ago."

"He spoke of no one else but you. His nervousness when he courted you after being friends for a long time, his pride at having you by his side. He loved your sense of humor, your wit, your intelligence, your ability to solve his puzzles. He admired your independence and your beauty. He called it 'a rare, wonderful combination.' You were paramount in his thoughts."

This was impossible. She knew Edgemont and this wasn't who he was.

"Are you sure we're speaking of the same man? Because that isn't at all what he led me to believe. It was quite the opposite."

"Edgemont was very good at what he did. In my eyes, and England's, he was the best. His last mission involved Napoleon. He was to root out his sympathizers. As a result, he received threats against his life many times. It's why he kept you at a distance. If others saw a loveless marriage, they wouldn't think to harm you.

"Before he went to Russia, he received threats involving you. He refused to leave you in England. He wouldn't go to Russia unless you were with him. Once he arrived, he wasn't comfortable especially when he was called away that night to the meeting."

"The night you were my bodyguard."

He bent his head down. She took a deep breath. He had more to tell her.

"There's more." He lifted his head and stared into her eyes. "Edgemont was killed leaving the palace after a meeting with the coalition ministers. He was murdered along with two others, my father and brother-in-law. For political reasons, no one was to know about the meeting or who attended. The report of his murder went along with the character he was supposed to have become."

Patrice was quiet. Was she relieved or angry? Neither. She was numb.

"My father, Leonid, and I played a dangerous game, straddling two sides of the fence. To others, my father and Leonid's services went to the highest bidder. I did not play that role. I remained the Tzar's man. Like me, their devotion was always to Russia, to the family.

"That night, the others went ahead while I finished my report. It was only luck that I too wasn't killed. That was when I vowed to bring the murderers to justice not only for the sake of Russia and the family, but also to restore Edgemont's reputation.

"To him, he played at being someone he wasn't. Because he plays games so well, he was believable. On the outside he was very convincing, but on the inside he was that boy that made up games to solve. I needed you to know the truth about Edgemont."

Patrice didn't know what to think or what to do. Nikolai got up to leave. She grabbed his hand and drew him back.

"Please, help me understand. Tell me about Edgemont."

He sat with her for the next two hours and told Patrice about his courage, his passion for his country, his devotion to her, and how he dared not write to her for fear someone would use the information and jeopardize her safety.

For some time, they sat and said nothing, letting her get used to who the real Edgemont was. Nikolai's version of the man she married aligned with the man who was her good friend.

"Excuse me, Lady Edgemont." Jean entered the room. "Lord Barrington is waiting. It's time to leave."

"Thank you, Jean."

On their ride to the dock, Patrice sat next to Nikolai. They didn't say anything. What would she say?

The dock was busy with activity. Not with passengers or commerce. It felt different. It felt ominous. It was a pressing fear, not for herself. She glanced at Nikolai, the only person she cared about. He helped her board the ship. The captain and crew were almost ready to sail.

Nikolai handed her a bundle. His fingers touched hers, creating a need to hold her. He resisted. He glanced at her face, her sweet face that he had dreamt about before they met, and told her more of the story.

"I told you Edgemont wouldn't send you anything for fear of compromising you. But that didn't mean he didn't write to you. I didn't think it wise. I was afraid it was too incriminating for him and you as well. I told him to burn it all, but he couldn't."

She silently encouraged him to go on.

"I see now why he saved them. They are a record of who he was and what he did. For him, with these letters he could hold onto you, not live the lie."

Reluctantly, he pulled his hand away. She stared at what was in her hands, then looked at him.

"In the bundle is his journal, a folio of documents, and letters addressed to you. Read them and understand the man."

"You are a true friend."

"That is the part of the story I couldn't tell you. Patrice, no matter what lies ahead, I will forever and always be your true friend."

He stared at her face not knowing if he would ever see her again. But he would remember her, always.

Nikolai turned and walked down the gangplank onto the dock. As the boat departed, he walked along the dock keeping Patrice in sight until he came to the end of the pier.

Patrice rushed between people as she hurried along toward the stern as the boat traveled on. At the stern she stood staring at Nikolai until the boat sailed around the bend.

Even then she didn't leave. She didn't move until Barrington came and fetched her.

# CHAPTER TWENTY-FOUR

THE SIX-DAY JOURNEY home gave Patrice time to grapple with the new information about Edgemont. Had she betrayed him by doubting him, by hating him, by not grieving for him? The decision to become a different person should never have been all his. She could present herself one way to the outside world, while remaining very different to those close to her. Her family prepared her well for that role.

She glanced out the carriage window. The coach turned onto the drive and in minutes they were under the portico. Emotionally drained and eager to get inside, Patrice removed the blanket from her lap. The coachman handed her down. She went to the door holding the unopened bundle of Edgemont's writings, and wondered about the revelations she held and how they would change her.

"Welcome home, Lady Edgemont."

Patrice stood in front of the opened door and stared at her butler.

"Mr. Regis?"

"May I take that?" He held out his hand for the package as she entered the foyer.

"That's quite all right." She hadn't let it out of her sight since Nikolai gave it to her. "Mr. Regis, I didn't expect you back until July. It's just March."

"Mrs. Regis and I came as soon as Mr. Carter sent word you returned home. Several staff have returned as well. Jean has returned from Ravencroft Hall. I expect the others by the end of the week." He signaled the footman to bring in her luggage.

"Thank you." She hurried into the library.

The room was clean, crisp, with a mildly nutty scent of newly polished furniture. A fire burned in the grate.

When she became mistress of The Mooring, she thought of this room as Edgemont's domain. The first few months they were married, they sat together in here after dinner. Sometimes to share a sherry. Sometimes to read a book. Sometimes to work out one of his puzzles.

Patrice put the bundle on the desk. The comfort of the room warmed her body and her soul. She let herself imagine those early months together with Edgemont and for a moment, felt the ghost of his presence.

*I need time to heal. I do mourn though, a bit for you, but mostly for us. For what might have been, and for that, I don't know if I can forgive you.*

Where to begin? She sat behind the desk, staring at the package, and wondered what he hid, what he thought, what he wanted, and if she was ready to face any of it.

"Good morning." Mrs. Regis entered and set tea, warm bread, and jam on the desk. "It's a cold morning. I can have breakfast for you."

"No. This is more than enough."

Mrs. Regis started to leave but hesitated at the door. "Lady Edgemont."

Patrice looked up and was struck by the flicker of apprehension that flashed across the housekeeper's face.

"It's good to have you home." The woman's tone was filled with determination as if she had been saving up to tell her.

"Thank you. It's good to be home. I'm glad you and the others have returned."

Patrice's face broke into a pleased smile at the pink tint on

Mrs. Regis' cheeks as she quietly left.

She poured her tea and while she stirred in sugar, she stared at the package. Was she brave enough to open it, read it, believe it?

For six days she dwelled on the picture Nikolai painted of Edgemont and how it differed from the one her husband had carefully crafted. Who did Edgemont fool? Her or Nikolai?

A dry, crackled laugh escaped her lips. Her judgement of men left much to be desired. Perhaps she should just give up. Not care.

She glanced out the window unable to look at the thing a moment longer. For a moment she thought to toss the whole thing into the fire. Why dredge up the past? What good would it do? He was gone.

Her eyes were drawn back to the bundle like a bee drawn to honey. Sitting there wrapped in brown paper and tied with a string, it looked innocent but had the potential of exposing the truth of the man, how he really felt, who he really was.

*Don't fear the truth.*

And don't live a lie. She let out a deep breath, pulled the package close, and tore off the wrapping. Inside was a plain box. Patrice opened the box and found a journal, a folio of papers, and stacks of letters neatly tied with string.

Patrice examined the black leather journal. There was nothing notable about it, no embossed name or family crest. She opened the cover and froze.

*On this, the twelfth day of the 3$^{rd}$ month of eighteen hundred and twelve I, Lord Benedict Edgemont, made Lady Patrice Montgomery my wife. Sape faqe qpsqyazf*

Reading Edgemont's message in his distinctive handwriting seemed to be an intrusion. The words were nothing out of the ordinary, but combined with his handwriting, she thought it was intimate. She heard his voice, his tone, the cadence of his speech that was uniquely his.

He never intended anyone to see this journal. The word

puzzle was a game he played when they were young. The fragment was his mark. Although she didn't recognize this one. She turned the page and was startled. Page after page was filled with random letters organized in columns.

"It's just like you Edgemont. Leave me with one of your unsolvable puzzles." In her head, she heard his chuckle.

*"It's solvable once you have the key. A good puzzle doesn't give up its answer easily. Keep looking. The key. The key unlocks the secret."*

Patrice rubbed her eyes and drained the last of the tea from her cup. She pulled out paper and a pencil and began to analyze the letters, as he had taught her.

Two hours later she sat back in the chair. The fact that the puzzle was one of Edgemont's letter substitution games was evident.

It had been so much easier when he helped her discover the answer. He had the key.

A glimmer of satisfaction warmed her face. The key. Putting the journal aside, she delved into the top desk drawer and looked through the papers. It wasn't there. She went through the next two drawers and still didn't find what she wanted.

Patrice took the folio out of the box. Perhaps he put the page here. She leafed through the folio surprised at what she found. Personal letters from several foreign ministers commending Edgemont's work with the phrases, lives saved, perseverance under fire, unique ability in the face of danger.

There weren't any documents like these in Edgemont's office. Had he removed them? A small voice in her head told her these citations had never been kept there, nor did he ever tell anyone about them. She replaced the documents in the folio and put it aside. An image was coming to light of a man who led two lives. One for the outside world and another filled with intrigue and danger.

She pressed both hands over her burning eyes. All that remained were the neatly tied stacks of letters addressed to her. Her heart raced at seeing her name in his handwriting. She wasn't ready for his words, not words intended only for her. Not yet.

If Nikolai was correct about Edgemont, then he assumed the role of a character specifically to attract particular people. He kept his distance from her to keep her safe. And when they killed him, people went to a great deal of trouble to explain his death away.

If she believed it, and she was beginning to think Nikolai told her the truth, why was he killed? What did he know? How would he protect it?

She picked up the journal. She read his message again. Her mind started to gather speed. The message in the journal was paramount. The puzzle had to be solved and with Nikolai away, the only person who could help her was Barrington. Patrice closed the box and put the journal into her reticule.

"Mr. Regis, the carriage, please. I'm going into the village."

✦

"PATRICE, THIS IS a pleasant surprise." Mrs. Bainbridge turned to her housekeeper. "Some tea, Ellen."

"I need to speak to Barrington or his brother. What is the fastest way to reach them?" She blurted out as she took a seat next to the headmistress.

"What has you so upset?" Mrs. Bainbridge put her hand on Patrice's arm, her voice sincere.

"Edgemont isn't what I thought he was."

"What did you think he was?" The question was innocent enough, but it was loaded with explosives.

"Not long after my marriage, he turned into someone who was not at all like the person I knew and who courted me. It made me believe our marriage was nothing but a sham. Now I find he was altogether a different person. Even his death. There was no mistress, only a dark alley in St. Petersburg and an," she paused, "assassination." The last word was barely a whisper.

Concern flickered in Mrs. Bainbridge's eyes. Patrice let out a breath. Maybe this wasn't as mad as it seemed.

"How have I not seen what is suddenly so obvious? Edgemont was everything I originally thought him to be. When we were younger his word puzzles were a game he played, we played together. It was something we always did, unimportant games we played even as we courted. We may have been playing unimportant games together, but he used them differently with others. They were his business. The word puzzles we played turned into something more serious. They were codes." She let out a deep breath and calmly said, "You see, he was a spy. That's why I need to speak to Barrington. He and Nikolai are the only ones I trust with this information. I've received a message from Edgemont."

"Message?" Mrs. Bainbridge gave her a pained look and put her arm around her. "Patrice, Edgemont is dead. He has been for almost a year."

Patrice took her husband's journal from her reticule.

"He left me his journal. That's where I found the message." She showed her the pages of random letters.

Mrs. Bainbridge stared at the pages. Finally, she glanced at Patrice an odd look on her face. "None of this makes sense. It's just random letters."

"Edgemont enjoyed puzzles. I thought at first that's all this was, but I went through his journal and now I think these pages with random letters are a message written in code. All I need is the key to solve it." A smile touched Patrice's face. *Keep looking for the key.* He said that all the time when we worked on his puzzles. Now his words keep echoing in my head."

Mrs. Bainbridge leafed through the pages. "There are scrambled words throughout the pages."

"Yes. I feel I am on the verge of an answer. Edgemont was close to Nikolai and both Barrington brothers. I can only hope that one of them has the secret to reading the code."

"Nikolai is fighting in Belgium and the Barringtons are on the continent as well. At the moment, all you can do is wait." Mrs.

Bainbridge closed the journal.

"Wait? Edgemont's business hid the fact that he was a spy. One of his clients was *Napoleon*. I am positive there is information here that is urgent. I must unravel the code. And he left me letters, ones he wrote to me but never sent. I haven't had the nerve to read them."

"What can you do at the moment but wait for Barrington?" Mrs. Bainbridge passed her a cup of tea, and after a thoughtful pause said, "And read Edgemont's letters. If not for his comments, then to see if the key to the code is there."

---

# CHAPTER TWENTY-FIVE

THAT EVENING, PATRICE had an informal dinner served in the breakfast room. She hardly tasted Mrs. Regis' food. She was preoccupied thinking about Mrs. Bainbridge's challenge.

She didn't have many choices. She could go to London and wait for the Barringtons, but that could take days, months even. Traveling to Belgium to locate Nikolai wasn't a choice at all. It was out of the question.

That left waiting in Sommer-by-the-Sea. Patrice let out a deep breath. So be it.

But she didn't have to be idle. There were a few things she could do.

She left her half-eaten dinner and retired to her room. Sitting at her writing desk, she penned a letter to Lord Edward Barrington to read when he returned. Her message was short, informing him of what she found and what she needed. If he didn't have the key, he might know who did.

Feeling better having taken some positive action, she proceeded to her next task. Edgemont's letters.

She opened the box and removed the first bundle. His writing style was familiar, both casual and friendly. He wrote as he spoke. It was as if he was standing in the room speaking to her.

*June 3, 1812*

*My dearest Patrice,*

*Today is a lovely day. A memory of our early days as faithful friends came to mind. I would like to walk with you along the cliffs as we used to before we were wed. Instead, I am in Spain.*

*I have a puzzle for you. It's at the bottom of this paper. There's nothing there, you say. Oh, my dear Patrice. There are lots of things you may not see, but I assure you, they are there.*

*—Edgemont*

The rest of the page was blank. She held it up to see if something was etched into the paper. Nothing. She held the paper at an angle looking for anything raised. She thought something was there but couldn't make it out. She held the parchment closer to the candle. Concentrating, straining to make out what was there. Slowly the letters darkened and as if by magic, words appeared.

*Yes, my dear. Invisible ink. As long as I have lemons, which are in abundance in Spain, we have our puzzle. Remember, a good puzzle doesn't give up its answer easily. Keep looking. The key. The key unlocks the secret.*

She read another.

*September 15, 1812*

*My dearest Patrice,*

*I have been traveling and will contact you as soon as I am able.*

*—Edgemont*

The rest of the paper was blank. She brought the page to the candle and watched the words appear.

*I'm in Moscow. The Russians will not give in to Napoleon. Fires have started, some say by the French, while others say by order of the Tzar. The wooden buildings are bursting into flames quickly. I see no way to save the city. It is a place without people, without supplies, and without food.*

*I am glad you cannot witness this and glad you are safe.*

One more letter, before she went to sleep.

*January 18, 1815*

*Dearest,*

*You were the most beautiful woman at the Ashcroft Gala this evening. I watched you from afar like a heart sick schoolboy rather than your husband. The one waltz I permitted myself was torture. To hold you in my arms and not crush you to my chest, not laugh, but play the disinterested husband.*

*—Edgemont*

She watched and wondered what his secret message would be. She lowered the paper when they appeared.

*But it is for you. To keep you safe. This is a small price to pay, one that I can and will make up to you.*

She returned the letters to the box. Friendship, hardship, and worship were themes of these messages. She wasn't certain, but thought Edgemont may have purposefully selected these to be the first letters for her to read. She closed the lid on the box. It was enough for one day.

As she readied herself for bed, she decided in addition to reading his letters she would search the library. Perhaps there was something there that could help her solve the puzzle.

⇥⟫⟩⟨⟪⇤

"LADY EDGEMONT." PATRICE looked down at her butler from atop the library ladder about to grab Julius Caesar's *De Bello Gallico*.

"Mrs. Bainbridge, Lady Euphemia, and Lady Harriet to see you."

"Thank you, Mr. Regis." The butler steadied the ladder. She

left the book in place thinking to take it later and came down from her perch. "Please have tea brought here today."

"You always did enjoy climbing." Mrs. Bainbridge handed her the post. "We come to you with your morning post. I hope we're not disturbing you."

Patrice was about to put the post on the desk when she noticed the letter was from Lord Edward.

"Not at all." Patrice gestured toward the chairs. She opened and read the letter. "God's big toe."

The women looked up at her. She kept reading.

"Patrice?" Mrs. Bainbridge spoke with an odd but gentle tone.

"Lord Edward thanks me for my concern and assures me he has all the important documents and information in hand." She lowered the document and stared blankly. "In a very kind way, Lord Edward Barrington has told me to mind my own business."

She tossed the letter onto the table as Mrs. Regis brought in tea. How could he dismiss her so off-handedly? How could he, sitting in the House of Lords, close to the issues in France and Russia, not be curious? She paced in front of the hearth. Perhaps she wasn't strong enough in her message. She halted. Yes, that must be it. If she couldn't count on him for help, she would take matters into her own hands.

"The devil with him. I'll solve the puzzle without his help." Patrice sat at the table, poured tea, and handed a cup to Mrs. Bainbridge.

"I'm sure he is just preoccupied at the moment," Mrs. Bainbridge said as she sipped. "I received a message from Reese and came right here. Napoleon marched into Paris with over 1,500 men. King Louis fled to Ghent."

"Surely, no one believed Napoleon left Elba to become a reclusive farmer." Effie looked at the plate of scones Mrs. Regis placed on the table.

"I agree." Mrs. Bainbridge put a splash of milk in her tea. "The Coalition is once again allied against Napoleon. Barrington had a message from Prince Blucher. Nikolai is commanding one of his divisions and is off to the front."

The silence was deafening. She had immersed herself with the puzzle and hadn't thought about Nikolai. Those odd moments before she fell asleep, when her defenses were down, he crept into her thoughts. She shifted her focus to the puzzle. Now she stirred her tea, the spoon hitting the side of the delicate cup. It was the only sound in the room.

Mrs. Bainbridge placed a gentle hand over hers. "You'll shatter the cup."

Patrice stopped, looked at the cup, then her friends.

"I can't sit and do nothing. I know Edgemont left me the journal for a reason." Patrice stood and paced in front of the window and stopped by the hearth. She glanced at them all.

"It could simply be a diary, written so no one can read it but him. You said he liked games." Hattie turned to Effie, then Mrs. Bainbridge, a worried expression on her face.

She hadn't noticed the concern on their faces until now. Did they all think she was mad? Her dead husband, whom she hated, had left her a coded message of some sort. God's middle toe. It *did* sound mad.

"You're probably right," she lied. They didn't understand. No one seemed to understand, except her. "I've been so away from society, what do you know of the new fashions? I need a new dress."

Patrice took her seat and for the next thirty minutes, they talked about the new fabric at the modiste. To Patrice they could have told her flour sacks were in fashion. It took every ounce of strength to keep her attention on the conversation.

"Thank you for your hospitality," Mrs. Bainbridge stood, a signal they were leaving. She went to the door as they filed out of the room. Mrs. Bainbridge was last.

"Patrice. We're all worried about you."

"I appreciate your concern. But you needn't worry."

Mrs. Bainbridge held her gaze for several heartbeats and finally smiled. "Come to the seminary during the week. I could use some company."

"Of course."

The headmistress caught up with Effie, and Hattie by the carriage.

Patrice noticed them shaking their heads and their worried expressions as the coachman handed them up. She was glad they called but in truth, she couldn't wait for them to leave. She needed to continue her search.

She loved them all, but no matter what they said, Edgemont's journal was in a code, and she planned to prove it.

⇒⇒⇒⟨⟨⟨

OVER THE NEXT weeks while the fighting continued on the continent with heavy casualties, Patrice scoured the library, declined her friend's invitations, and yelled at Edgemont in absentia, Prince Blucher's army was near defeat and Wellington was suffering.

Patrice had gone through most of the library, but she was unwilling to give up.

"Edgemont. It's here somewhere." She stared at the book-plate as if Edgemont's handwriting would twist and turn into the answer.

She stared at the jumbled letters *sape faqe qpsqyazf.* It had to be a letter substitution. She wrote out the alphabet A through Z. Edgemont shifted everything three places. A became D. She substituted the letters of the first four letters and got vdsh. Meaningless.

Edgemont had told her that the most used letter in the English language was E. Trusting Edgemont, she decided to count the number of times each letter of the alphabet appeared in the first three journal pages. The letter Q appeared most often.

She wrote the jumbled word *sape faqe qpsqyazf* on a paper and circled the three Qs. Over them she put an E.

"God's toes, Edgemont."

Disheartened, she wrote her plea on the next line and stared at the paper. Her heart thudded. She sat up and looked more closely. It couldn't be that simple.

She substituted the letter S in the code with the letter G. She knew the letter belonged there and her heart raced faster. Quickly, she replaced the E with S. It all fit.

Without stopping, she wrote the letters A through Z. Beneath the letter A she put the letter O, and beneath the letter P she put the letter D. Then she counted the number of letters between the actual letter and the substitute. There were twelve between each set of letters. Her hand shook as she mapped the rest of the substitute letters. Finally, she stared at the results, her breath coming in spurts.

"God's toes Edgemont." She let out a throaty laugh filled with relief and elation. He used her epithet as his key. She should have realized twelve was the number. It was their special number.

She forced herself to settle down and spent the next hour and a half solving the rest of the puzzle. As the words began to flow, she got more excited. The urgency of the information came into view as she transcribed the letters. This information had to go to Barrington at once.

"Are you taking callers?" Barrington stood at the doorway, his coat over his arm and a scowl on his face.

"Barrington? I was just thinking I needed to see you. When did you arrive home?"

"Earlier this morning. A note from Honoria was waiting for me. I'll get right to the point, Patrice. Honoria and the other ladies are concerned. You have not been out of the house in days and when they come and call here, you're preoccupied with the library." He gestured at the walls of books.

"Yes, yes, but I can explain." She could kiss Mrs. Bainbridge for getting Barrington here.

"You are a bright, intelligent woman. That you pieced together what Edgemont was about is more than commendable, but if you think he—"

"I know what Edgemont wanted to tell us." The calmness in her voice contradicted the excitement bursting inside her. She heard his quick inhale.

"What do you mean?" Barrington stood there, challenging her for an answer.

"Exactly what I said. I solved the puzzle in his journal." She held up the book. "It's a map of locations where Napoleon's supplies can be found."

Barrington took the journal from her and scanned the pages.

"He doesn't use place names. He uses the longitude and latitude." Patrice watched the frustration build on Barrington's face and knew he didn't have the key.

"I'm not surprised." He handed the book back to her. "He's done that in the past. According to him, it's more exact. To him, it was a game, and he certainly enjoyed his games. I don't see anything recognizable in his journal."

She gave him her transcription. Barrington's eyes widened as he quickly read the pages.

"You're certain about this information." It was more a statement than a question. He didn't give her time to respond. "You are just as clever as Edgemont. You've done very well."

"*Edgemont* did well. All I did was solve his game."

"War is a deadly game. Edgemont may not have been a soldier, but in many ways he was the game master. I'll get these to my brother at once." He put the pages in his pocket. A look of admiration flashed across his face. "Regarding my reason for coming, I'll report back to Honoria that all is well." His eyes took on a softer look, the look that went with unpleasant news.

"Is there something else?" She held her breath, almost afraid to hear what he had to say.

"No, not at all. You're very good at solving puzzles."

"I'm just as good at creating them. It's all about the key." The admiration she saw in his eyes was gratifying.

Barrington hesitated before he turned to leave. "I will let my brother know." He gave her a nod and was gone.

Patrice sat back, exhausted, but satisfied.

"You were correct, Edgemont. The key *is* the secret." She went to the window and stared at the maze. "All around, your puzzles were the answer. I thank you for teaching me to persevere. To find the answers. Thank you, my friend. I hope now you can rest in peace."

⚜

# CHAPTER TWENTY-SIX

IT WAS A mild day for the end of July. Patrice had read all of Edgemont's letters. They made her laugh, think deeply, and at times, cry. Now, it was time to put the past to rest. She tied up the letters with a satin ribbon and put them away with his journal in a safe place.

With the help of her friends and Barrington, they celebrated his life by saying good-bye at a small graveside ceremony with refreshments at the tearoom.

While they settled and waited for tea to be served, Patrice's mind was somewhere else. She hadn't stopped thinking about Nikolai. For three months she vigilantly read notices of the Waterloo dead and wounded. There wasn't any word. Barrington couldn't help her either. As the last of the soldiers arrived home, she gave up hope of his return.

"Patrice." She turned to Barrington. "Keep the good memories, the ones where you both enjoyed and loved each other. Be proud of his accomplishments in business and his service to the country. As I know he is of yours."

Patrice smiled nervously, not knowing if he meant Edgemont or Nikolai. "Thank you for your kind words."

"My brother sends you his warm wishes as well. You deciphered the code—"

"Edgemont deciphered the code. Not me."

"As you wish," he nodded and raised his cup in salute. "Either way he is grateful to the Edgemonts. He would like you to consider working with him. Your persistence to find the solution even though you were not encouraged is more than admirable. He is sincere. I hope you will consider his offer."

She was too startled by his words to speak. He waited patiently.

"I received Lord Edward's message earlier this week. His words were humbling. I appreciated them, but they weren't necessary. I completed Edgemont's final task. In the process, I learned," she paused as she remembered all that had happened, all the misconceptions that had to be corrected, "I learned another side of the man that he kept hidden from me. What I am saying is we both benefited.

"Lord Edward asked under what conditions I would work for him. I'm drafting that now. Once it is complete, I will send him my response."

"I am pleased you are considering the position. Please call on me if you need any assistance dealing with Lord Edward. I know how to get his attention. You will not regret working with him and the others."

Barrington turned toward Mrs. Bainbridge, who had leaned close to whisper in his ear.

Patrice had spoken with Barrington many times. He was welcome at the seminary and a close friend of Mrs. Bainbridge. The looks between the two spoke for themselves. But she had never heard him speak from his heart as he had at Edgemont's graveside.

She respected the private man, his opinions, and his sincerity. Today he spoke with emotion and caring she had never seen before. Accepting his brother's offer was on her lips, but she thought it best to tell Lord Edward first and not offend him, that much she knew about him.

Patrice freshened her cup of tea and turned to Effie. "Would you care for more?" She glanced at Effie with the pot in her hand.

Effie's gaze was elsewhere.

"What are you staring at?"

"A gentleman Tanya is speaking to. She has the most interesting guests. See for yourself."

"No. You tell me what he looks like." She picked up her cup.

"He has a commanding way about him, tall, muscular." Effie tilted her head, judging the man.

"How do you know that?" Effie seemed to be enjoying the game, so Patrice decided to humor her.

"From the way his coat pulls across his chest and the narrowness of his hips." Effie leaned close to her. "If you doubt my description, you can turn around and see for yourself."

"No, no, go right ahead." Patrice waved her hand, a dismissive gesture. "You're doing a fine job."

"As I was saying, tall, muscular, narrow hips, a neatly trimmed beard, short hair with the hint of a wave. Wait a minute." She squinted her eyes then glanced at Patrice. "Ah, yes. He has summer-sky blue eyes."

Patrice blinked several times, taking in what Effie said. She stared at her friend, who nodded toward the door.

Patrice dared not turn around. "God's toes, where is he now?" She could hardly get her voice to work.

"Behind you, Lady Edgemont."

Patrice closed her eyes as the soft, mellow voice caressed her. In a single movement she was out of her seat and spun around. He stood inches away. Her feelings were a crosscurrent of emotions. She was thrilled, concerned, relieved, and scared.

"Lady Edgemont." He dipped his head, his eyes never left her. "How good to see you again."

His fixed gaze held her captive. He tilted his head in that arrogant yet elegant nod he did so well, sending ripples of excitement dancing over her.

"Your Grace, how good it is to see you. I'm glad you're safe."

His face lit in a smile, the one that warmed her to her core and left her damp.

He leaned close to her. "Will you introduce me to your friends? I didn't have the opportunity to meet them the last time I was in Sommer-by-the-Sea."

Her friends? She turned to them and for the moment was surprised they were there. She took a deep breath, but that didn't quiet her heart from racing or the excitement that washed over her in waves.

"Your Grace, I would like to introduce you to my dear friends, Lady Marianna Ravencroft, Lady Euphemia Brandt, Lady Harriet Manning, and Mrs. Honoria Bainbridge. You know Lord Barrington.

"Ladies, I would like to introduce you to Grand Duke Nikolai Antonovich Baranov of the House of Breuce."

"Baranov, come and join us." Barrington motioned to an empty seat next to Patrice.

Her friends bombarded Nikolai with questions. She didn't hear them. Her body tingled, her stomach rebelled, and her eyes never left him. All the waiting. All the worrying. All the hoping. He came back to her.

"Patrice." She looked up at Mrs. Bainbridge. "It's a lovely day. Why don't you take His Grace for a walk along the beach? He's been gracious to answer all our questions, that isn't why he came to our table."

"Thank you, Mrs. Bainbridge." Nikolai stood and offered Patrice his arm. "Shall we, Lady Edgemont?"

She didn't speak, just stood, and put her arm through his.

"Ladies, Barrington." Nikolai put his hand over hers and led Patrice away.

They walked through the village to the cliff path. It gave her time to get her breath back.

"You grew back your beard."

"You sound disappointed."

She glanced at him. "Not at all. It reminds me of *moy lev*."

She kept walking but heard the catch in his breath.

"Summer-sky blue eyes?"

"You were eavesdropping." She couldn't hide the smile in her voice.

"I was standing behind you." He gave her a guilty, little-boy look that was out of character for the prince that stood beside her. "I couldn't help hearing what she said."

At the cliff, her gaze moved along the sandy shore to the breaking waves. She led him down the path to the beach. They strolled on until they came to the boulders and bend in the coastline.

"I went through Edgemont's papers. At first, I wasn't sure if I was angry or glad that you gave them to me."

He didn't say anything.

"When I finished reading the last letter, I was angry at him for not telling me what he was doing or why. All along I thought it was me. Something I did, something I lacked.

"I came to a different conclusion after reading them. It may seem strange, but I think he knew the outcome. I don't think he was assassinated as much as he gave himself up. I don't think he saw any other way for the game to end that wouldn't cost him dearly. It's why he wouldn't burn his journal, the citations, and his letters. Edgemont was a very brave man." Her voice trailed to a whisper.

"He had been a good friend for so long, my parents thought it would be the perfect marriage. I adored him as a friend."

"But?" Nikolai's single word said it all.

"Some friends are just that. Friends. He was aware of my feelings and still wanted to marry me."

She stood by his side, felt the light wind whipping at their clothes, listened to the seabirds squawking overhead, and gazed at the pounding surf pummeling the shore.

"I've worried about you." It was the only thing she could think to say.

"As friends do." His voice was soft, almost apologetic.

Her breath was suddenly strained, as though someone tightened the laces of her stays, making it impossible for her to breathe. The storm of emotions Nikolai set off with a nod, a look, a touch, frightened and thrilled her at the same time. She didn't want him to be her friend, not that way.

He let out a breath.

"I won't deny the battles were bloody. Everyone was disheartened when Prince Blucher failed. I was caught with my men behind enemy lines.

"That didn't stop us from our mission. I took my best men and made sure Napoleon's supplies never reached him. I owe you a great deal of thanks. From the precision of the information, I knew you had solved Edgemont's puzzle. I wasn't surprised."

"Barrington and Lord Edward have asked for my assistance. I'm considering it."

Nikolai turned and stared at her. Emotions flashed across his face.

The bottom fell out of her stomach as the undeniable and dreadful facts surfaced. He was here for Edgemont, not for her. She contemplated continuing Edgemont's work as a means of remaining close to Nikolai. Was it a foolish idea?

She lowered her head as she struggled to keep the tears from falling and him from seeing her chin quivering.

Her first instinct was to leave, get as far away from him as possible. There was nothing to be gained by staying. She glanced at the path. If she left now, they could both part as friends.

"*Lishichka.*"

Little fox. She closed her eyes tight at his tender tones.

He lifted her chin with the crook of his finger.

"Don't leave."

Her eyes flew open as she realized their connection had been so complete, he knew her thoughts.

"Leave? All I want is to *stay* with you. Be with you."

She took his face in her hands, kissed his lips, and stepped back. "I wanted to do that the first time I saw you at the tearoom. It was an unfulfilled, overpowering urge."

Slowly, a dangerous playful smile lit his face. His eyes turned dark with a passion she had only dreamt of. He didn't say anything for several heartbeats.

"Patrice." He drew out the syllables of her name. "It was the same for me." His deep voice simmered with barely checked passion. "Do you remember when I escorted you in St. Petersburg?"

"When you were my bodyguard."

"Yes. That was when I learned everything Edgemont told me about you was true. I already had developed an affection for you, but that evening." He looked at the ground. "That evening I fell in love with you."

Patrice lifted his face. She saw the man who escorted her to the ballet and dinner and taught her how to drink vodka.

He put something in her hand.

She stared at the Royal Brooch then gave him a questioning look.

"This is my family's heirloom, not the Tzar's. It is given to the eldest son, a symbol of his position in the family. The Baranov Brooch is a gift the eldest son gives to his bride."

A riot of emotions ran through her at the idea he loved her.

"God's toes, *Lishichka*. I love you. Marry me."

Nikolai drew her close. There was something perfect about being in his arms. With him she was safe, complete.

He tipped her chin up, stared into her eyes, then lowered his head. Her eyes fluttered closed, with anticipation. Her body throbbed with desire.

"Look at me." His command was gentle but firm. "For months I've imagined your red hair and green eyes. Your lips. You're funny, God's toes. I've missed it all. Once I realized you had solved the puzzle, I had this mad idea we could solve any puzzle as long as we did it together."

"Lord Edward has asked me to work for him."

"What are your terms?" Nikolai's voice was low and confident, but underneath she still heard the silky passion.

"That I will only work for him if I can work with you."

Nikolai exhaled a long-contented sigh.

"I should marry you, if only to prove Tanya wrong."

He gave her a quizzical look.

"According to the tea leaves, I am to marry a man whose name begins with H."

Nikolai threw his head back, laughing so hard he had a difficult time catching his breath.

"What's so funny?"

He bent down and wrote his name in the sand. In Cyrillic, Николай. He pointed to the letters and said his name, Nikolai.

They stared into each other's eyes. Her body ached for him with a sudden fierce fire that she willingly embraced.

The tenderness and passion in his gaze drove her on. She could feel his uneven breathing on her cheek as he held her close. His hand found the hollow of her back and drew her closer. She didn't resist.

She wasn't sure who closed the distance between them. All that mattered was, when their lips tenderly touched, her stomach was sent into a spin.

The sensation as his tongue traced her lips had her dizzy. She gasped as he nipped, then soothed them with small kisses.

He parted from her by a few inches, but she would have none of that. She reclaimed his lips and was rewarded with his slow, tender kisses.

His spell was cast. He kissed her lips, her ear, the side of her neck. He hesitated but a moment before he kissed the base of her throat. He was still too far away, so she put her arms around his neck and drew him closer, reveling in the sensation, the desire.

"*Lishichka*. Will you be mine?"

"Yes, *moy lev*. Forever and always."

## THE END

# About the Author

There was never a time when *USA Today* Bestseller, RUTH A. CASIE hasn't had a story in her head. When she was little, she and her older sister would dress up and act out the ones Ruth creative. Today, Ruth writes exciting and beautifully told legendary historical romances that are both rich and engaging. Her stories feature strong women and the men who deserve them, endearing flaws and all. Her stories are full of, 'edge of your seat' suspense, mind-boggling drama, and a forever-after romance.

She lives in New Jersey with her hero, three empty bedrooms and a growing number of incomplete counted cross-stitch projects. Before she found her voice, she was a speech therapist (pun intended), client liaison for a corrugated manufacturer, and vice president at an international bank where she was a product/ marketing manager, but her favorite job is the one she's doing now—writing romance. Ruth hopes her stories become your favorite adventure.

Fun facts about Ruth:

1. She filled her passport up in one year.
2. She has three series. The Druid Knight is a time travel romance. The Stelton Legacy is a historical fantasy about the seven sons of a seventh son. Havenport Romances are contemporary romantic suspense stories. She also writes for the Pirates of Britannia connected world.

3. She did a rap with her son to "How Many Trucks Can a Tow Truck Tow If a Tow Truck Could Tow Trucks."

4. When she cooks she dances around the kitchen.

5. Her sudoku books is in the bathroom and that's all she'll say about that!

### Social Media Links:

Website:
ruthacasie.com

Instagram:
instagram.com/ruthacasie

Facebook private reader's page, Casie Café:
facebook.com/groups/963711677128537

Facebook Author Page:
facebook.com/RuthACasie

Twitter:
twitter.com/RuthACasie

BookBub:
bookbub.com/authors/ruth-a-casie

Amazon:
amazon.com/author/ruthacasie

Goodreads:
goodreads.com/author/show/4792909.Ruth_A_Casie

YouTube:
bit.ly/3hI5eQr

www.ingramcontent.com/pod-product-compliance
Lightning Source LLC
Chambersburg PA
CBHW070944190726
48292CB00004B/1327